Period Pieces

Other books by March Cost

Period Pieces
by March Cost

Chilton Books
a division of Chilton Company . Publishers
Philadelphia / New York

To: John Inglis Morrison

Everything dates but devotion—
These period pieces come with mine

Acknowledgments

I am deeply indebted to Siegfried Sassoon for permission to quote from his poem "Silent Service" in *The Mask*.

Third Class to Joy. Copyright 1935 by March Cost.
Reprinted by permission of *The Glasgow Herald*.

Master Craftsman. Copyright 1949 by March Cost.
Reprinted by permission of *The Weekly Scotsman*.

Man of the Moment. Copyright 1954 by March Cost.
Reprinted by permission of *The Evening Standard*.

Contents

Period Pieces

The Christmas Angel

The Christmas Angel

Her safety was threatened. It happened every Christmas. And this year she had not taken the usual precautions. Freedom was her treasured possession, her fortress a small suite in the best hotel in this large spa, for Mrs. Debrett enjoyed life. A rich widow of fifty, she felt and looked agreeably like forty. Mr. Debrett had been a distinct trial, and forty was the age at which Mrs. Debrett had belatedly blossomed—with no relatives . . . and a limited number of acquaintances, all now under suitable control. People were so liable to pounce! And Mrs. Debrett, resolutely at large, declined to be tied. Her last-minute arrangements, her spasmodic plans were put down to impulse. They were, in fact, a deliberate strategy to leave herself uncommitted. If Conscience whispered: "Anti-social?" Mrs. Debrett could as swiftly retort: "Remember Dudley!" and silenced, but not satisfied, Conscience would retire. Not that Mrs. Debrett cared two straws. Peace was all she craved —and her own way at last. In Dudley she had an alibi to sanction any self-absorption. Only at Christmas did suspicion suggest that freedom might yet prove another word for boredom. Hitherto,

(3

tropical cruises and long-distance air flights had enabled her to take Christmas in her stride, but this year it had caught her out. Senseless to advertise her isolation by dining in the hotel restaurant! And only a degree livelier to eat her Christmas Eve dinner in her suite, where if she pulled the hotel cracker by herself, dementia might at least vary proceedings!

No, she must lose herself in that gigantic dinner-dance-cabaret show at the Majestic, where mercifully she knew nobody. It was only a matter of time, and Christmas would be over. . . .

The marble entrance of the Majestic was congested. Guests streamed up a mirrored stairway, holly-wreathed tonight. Music increased this bustling festivity. But a blow awaited Mrs. Debrett—

"Madam, a table for one is impossible tonight. On the telephone we confirmed one *cover*."

Mrs. Debrett knew when she was beaten—it was one of her charms. She gave a careless nod. "But madam can rest assured —another lady will be present."

Amused, she followed the maître d'hôtel across the crowded gold and green restaurant, to an empty table set for four.

Calmly Mrs. Debrett seated herself. She had a pale face with nondescript features, but she dressed with style and discretion. Her frock was the fashionable African-violet color—of a muted shade. It imposed itself stealthily yet irresistibly—as Mrs. Debrett herself was inclined to do.

Almost at once a waiter had bowed a thin, middle-aged man to the chair opposite. This guest had a dry, tanned face with a meager but military mustache. He bowed to Mrs. Debrett without enthusiasm, and took his place with reserve. Bachelor, Mrs. Debrett decided, with a certain sympathy. She was further disarmed by the undeniable shabbiness of his well-tailored lounge suit. His black tie was striped with three incisive colors. She felt she should have placed those clues, but could not. His hands, as he took the menu, were worn but rather beautiful. A surgeon perhaps—Indian Medical Service? Yet something had clearly intervened before final achievement. She feared he had ceased to operate while still gazetted Major! Today the world made a fetish of youth.

To confirm this, a young man, protesting quite loudly, was refusing to sit down beside them. A handsome young man who scarcely knew what to do with his exceptional height. A shy young man whose anxiety was explosive.

Smiling inflexibly, the maître d'hôtel insisted: "I can assure you, sir, it is better to sit down. The lady is bound to inquire for you. She will be shown here at once. We have your name: Mr. Robert Yule."

"But you haven't got hers—and in that infernal crush . . ." He had an unabashed Glasgow accent.

"Miss Sandra Jevons—you have already given it, sir!" Adroitly the maître d'hôtel vanished.

The young man sat down heavily, with a hunted look at his two companions. His chair seemed wholly inadequate.

"Abject!" he told them. "Not meeting her in the hall. But they insisted I moved on."

"Ladies are often late," bleakly the Major smiled.

Graciously, Mrs. Debrett amended: "She will understand."

"Talk of angels . . ." and the Major nodded. "Here I think she comes!"

Turning, Mrs. Debrett had her first glimpse. The dinner orchestra itself appeared to pause an instant. As one man, the guests crowding adjoining tables glanced up, paused, and worshipped.

A vision of loveliness was about to cross the ballroom floor, flanked by receptionist and maître d'hôtel. The angel advanced slowly in an ankle-length ballet frock of heat-haze blue, the color of a summer sky. At her shoulders transparent net was seasonably sprinkled with chenille snow flakes. Her radiant hair was fair enough to seem frosted in artificial light. The sweetness of her expression was the inevitable outcome of perfection, but it caught the observer's breath. This was not simply another pretty girl—it was beauty herself. Mrs. Debrett was the first to recover.

The young man arose, stumbling in his haste. *"Angel,"* he breathed, oblivious of all else.

The angel had a very gentle voice. Tiny, in fact. "Oh, Robbie!" she said, but that was all he needed. Her heavenly blue eyes tenderly included his companions. In a little gesture of caress, or blessing, she extended her hand—

"This must be your aunt and uncle?"

"No, no!" Robbie was again distraught. "The place is full. This lady and gentleman have proved agreeable—that is to say, we're sharing with them. The table I mean. When you found you *could* come, there wasn't time to rebook."

Nobody paid the slightest attention. Fascinated, those at the adjoining tables were watching the angel seat herself, for the nearer she approached, the more exquisite she grew. Her every movement suggested that time had stopped and eternity begun—rather like a slow-motion picture bent on prolonging wonder. Mrs. Debrett did indeed wonder what would happen in this wicked world if the angel ever had to whisk an egg. And to restore illusion, she glanced across at the Major.

To Mrs. Debrett's surprise, the Major was frowning. This struck her as odd. The army should be at home with beauty—not so enthusiastically perhaps as the navy, but certainly at ease.

Promptly, Mrs. Debrett heard herself announce: "Champagne is indicated, I think. I hope you will all give me the pleasure of joining me in mine."

"A sound idea!" The speed of the Major's response somewhat startled Mrs. Debrett. He was a male recipient, after all. Yet such was his authority that she felt obliged to overlook this.

"*Champagne!*" the angel turned a lustrous look on her benefactors. "And for us too? Robbie, isn't this kind?"

"Rather!" the young man moved uneasily in his chair. "But a bit of an imposition, sir. After all, we are strangers to you and your wife."

"No, this is Christmas. . . ." Hastily Mrs. Debrett signaled: "*Waiter!*" and, to the sardonic amusement of the Major, secured instant attention. Despite a false start, the table was well and truly launched at last.

Except for the angel. She was declining soup. So prettily that the waiter thought that she desired it. The Major and Robbie, momentarily unaware, ate theirs with gusto. Tiresomely, Mrs. Debrett felt a twinge of compassion. When last had these two men had a square meal?

Someone at the next table exclaimed: "The good old Majestic may be a bit of a free-for-all, but its cuisine is still first rate." Mrs. Debrett was inclined to agree. She too had finished her soup—

The angel, however, was feeling the heat oppressive. This robust revelry belonged to another clime!

"You *look* delightfully cool," Mrs. Debrett assured her.

Unhappily, the angel next discovered, on coming finally to earth, that her napkin was missing.

"Waiter!" fruitlessly Robbie waved—he almost arose. "A serviette!"

"Oh *Robbie!*" the angel whispered, with a look of ineffable anguish. "You promised that you'd remember. *Napkin,* always!"

"Sorry, darling." Robbie had flushed to his eyebrows. He looked so fiercely mortified that Mrs. Debrett's hard heart smote her.

Distinctly she said: "Waiter—I've dropped mine as well. A *serviette* for me also."

An unholy light leapt in the Major's eye. The waited misread it. "And you, sir?"

Piously, the Major replied: "I *have* my serviette."

Dazed, the angel gazed into space, and as the waiter, a raw recruit, helpfully flipped her napkin open, he swept her bread roll into her lap. Together he and the angel bent to correct this crime. Their heads crashed.

"*Hell!*" moaned the angel, and Mrs. Debrett feared she had decided to faint. Their adjoining neighbors ceased to eat. All present participated in the disaster. The angel opened her forget-me-not eyes on the faithful. With a divine simplicity she agreed that she was still present.

Sole Veronique and Paul Roget helped to restore equilibrium, although the angel was obliged to reject the turkey that followed. For the first time a trace of sternness outlined her cupid's-bow mouth. But heaven, Mrs. Debrett reflected, was bound to be vegetarian.

Revelation was indeed swift. The angel announced: "I'd much rather have a steak, Robert. Underdone."

A look of unmatched horror flashed across Robert's face.

Smoothly the Major said: "A la carte dishes take thirty minutes here. Tonight it might be longer."

Mesmerically, the angel looked at the Major—the celestial blue of her gaze inscrutable. Then she turned to discover that the maître d'hôtel had materialized instead of that half-baked waiter.

"Turkey," she conceded. "Just what you would know."

That amount, on the angel's plate, proved to be negligible, and in silent congratulation the Major and Mrs. Debrett kept up a careless exchange. Every word from their companions was an additional bond.

"Oh, Robbie," the angel was confessing, "if you only knew —it was agony to get here."

"Terribly sorry, darling," glumly, adoringly he listened.

"Mummy's on Daddy's side now. I'm simply *torn*. And she made me promise, before I left, to go on to my aunt's party later."

"*No!*" forcibly Robbie jerked back his chair—its legs protesting.

"Just a token appearance, darling. The party is at the White Hussar—no distance at all. I'll stay here as long as I can, of course."

For the first time Robbie showed fight. "Sandra, you can't!"

"Yes, darling—but only for supper-dance. It's been a dreadful day. Don't spoil this happy hour."

Robert glowered. "First you couldn't, then you could! I just wish I'd known this earlier. Now, I've left Bess alone in that boardinghouse. And at the last minute too. I feel a perfect swine."

"Oh, Robbie, I'm sorry! Did—did she say anything?"

"No, only looked."

"Oh, poor you! I think that's worse. Much meaner, really."

"Bess mean?" his laugh was more of a bark. "If you'd ever met my sister, you'd know what rot that was."

"But, Robbie, you told me she *had* to study—that her language degree came first."

"Not on Christmas Eve!" His voice hardened. "She'd bought a new frock too. I can't understand your parents blowing hot and cold like this."

Reproachfully, the angel whispered, "Robbie, how *can*

you be so cruel? You know I'm all they've got. Their only child. Oh, I could run a thousand miles!"

Blandly Mrs. Debrett and the Major were traveling too. Tactfully remote, they were now in Rhodesia. Even there, the angel's voice, small but insistent, reached them. The Major recognized it as a precision instrument.

"Daddy's done all he could. He's offered you a job. In the London store too. It's *you* who are to blame, Robbie! Hesitating like this."

"Sandra, I'm aiming to be an electrical engineer."

"And just *where* has that got you, darling?"

Even in Rhodesia, the question gave them pause. But Robbie blundered on: "Hang it all, I'm just at the beginning!"

"You've said it, Robbie! That's why Daddy is paving the way."

Belligerently Robbie muttered: "So I'm to throw away my National Certificate—am I?"

"Well, darling, what's it leading to, after all?"

Icily the young man said: "My Higher National Certificate, of course."

"But in between you haven't got a job. That's Daddy's point. There's nothing in it. Financially, I mean."

Doggedly the young man said: "We can wait—like other people. I mean to go on the sandwich-system. Equal periods spent at university and the works."

A sandwich-system! In Singapore, Mrs. Debrett herself felt apprehensive. On a qualm she fled to Florida. But the Major did not follow. Robbie had intervened. Outraged, the young man was challenging his seniors, with the help of Paul Roget:

"Nothing in engineering, sir! Can you beat that?"

Gloomily, the Major shook his head. "Takes time, you

know. And time tells on a woman. They're born for something better."

The angel brightened. As a flower, sunwards, she unfolded to the Major: "That's what Mummy says! It's all too ghastly. Engineers are almost bound to go abroad. Imagine the Colonies! Australia, for instance, where only the rim is cultivated. Robert might easily be sent to the interior with his cables. In the interior we could vanish. Not even our bodies to be found!"

Grimly, the Major agreed: "Yours never would be."

Angrily, the young man glared. Plum pudding, blazing with brandy was drawn alongside—fuel to fire.

Apprehensively, the angel drew back. "I shall have an ice."

Their waiter, that raw recruit, his face streaming with sweat, bent over her. Hoarsely, but hospitably he said: "You can have plum pudding as well as the ice, miss. It's included tonight."

The angel shuddered. "Neither—thank you. But a glass of water . . . right away!"

Valiantly the waiter stretched out a forbidden arm, and removed a jug of iced water from the next table. In his haste to oblige, he caught his foot on the abandoned trolley, but steadied himself miraculously, and poured the water, neatly enough, down the angel's back.

With a yelp that froze the assembly, she sprang to her feet—then sank back in sobs. Chaos reigned. On every side, her neighbors rose to attention. But only for seconds. At once the Majestic took command. The orchestra redoubled its efforts. Another contingent of waiters was rushed to the front. The scene of calamity was cordoned off by messengers of appeasement. A spotless towel was proffered in truce. A page appeared with a fan on a salver. And the maître d'hôtel, that seasoned campaigner, having brought up his reinforcements at the double, decided upon deployment.

Solicitously he addressed Mrs. Debrett: "Madam is also wet!"

Shamelessly, Mrs. Debrett deserted to the enemy, for at this stage a devil entered her. It was years since *she* had been an angel—

"The merest nothing!" deliberately she smiled. Mrs. Debrett's teeth were always a surprise. Not only were they flawless, they were also her own. Her smile transformed her face as sunlight bewitches a landscape. Mrs. Debrett did not smile often. Newcomers had been known to succumb to the smile at sight— and, of course, all that Mrs. Debrett desired was to be left alone.

But now she smiled . . . and charm, order, and elegance were restored. Nothing else was of the slightest importance. Harmony alone existed. Relieved, the staff withdrew.

Sandra herself caught that siren flash. Her sniffs ceased: "No, Robbie, *please* don't come! It's been such a shock I must go home. *They'll* get me a taxi. And you've got to pay the bill—"

Sternly the young man addressed the Major. "I shall be back in a few minutes—Please tell the waiter . . ."

"Well, well, well!" Mrs. Debrett said softly as the lovers disappeared. "Isn't youth a sad time? What a blessing to have outgrown one's heart! Now his night is in ruins."

"Better that than his life," the Major said callously.

"Oh, I agree," and irrepressibly Mrs. Debrett began to laugh. "In fact, I once behaved almost as badly as Sandra in a similar predicament."

The Major's cold eye gleamed. "Is it too much to ask how that story ended?"

"In the worst possible way. I apologized. He forgave me. It is sometimes fatal to marry your first love."

He nodded, amused. "I too made the same mistake. How long did *your* martyrdom last?"

"Fifteen years." She paused. "And yours?"

"Twenty—" he broke off. Robert Yule was shouldering his way back to them.

Stiffly the young man said: "I must apologize. We've pretty well spoiled your dinner. Strangers too."

"Sit down," the Major told him, "and listen to me. . . . About that sandwich course—you'd better call on me next week. Here's my card."

The young man took the card, read it, stared.

"I can't believe it," he said stupidly. "It's just not possible. Do you mean to say . . . ?"

"Just that."

Robert continued to stare. Gone were the ardor and anxiety which the angel had inspired. His harassed young face registered a growing bliss—the Major might have been the pearly gates.

"Well, I'm blowed!" he declared. "The first electrical engineer in the U.K. Randolph Rennie of *Refrigeration United!*"

But Mrs. Debrett had stiffened. There was a certain valuable block of shares in Refrigeration United which she herself possessed. Yet she felt hoaxed. The shabby man beside her, so painstakingly groomed that he aroused compassion, was a millionaire.

Eagerly Robbie was amplifying: "That new balloon-type door gasket—" Mrs. Debrett almost took off herself. "Why, sir, your competitors are defrosting at sight!" His face as suddenly clouded. "And I've wasted the whole evening—"

Briskly Mr. Rennie said: "There's tomorrow—or rather next week. Now, hop into a taxi and fetch Bess. We'll meet you at the White Hussar in an hour."

"*We?*" Mrs. Debrett ironically raised an eyebrow.

"Madam," Mr. Rennie frowned, "you have made my evening. If you fail me now, I shall never forgive you."

"But isn't this Mrs. Rennie?" Robbie expostulated.

Stifling a laugh, she admitted: "No, this is Edith Debrett. And of course I'll be charmed to welcome Bess. Perhaps *she* is the Christmas angel we've all been looking for!"

But Robbie had one more anxiety. "Her new dress isn't a dance frock—we don't get around very much. It's an afternoon black two-piece."

"Black is always *de rigueur*," Edith Debrett assured him, and raised her cigarette for a light.

Robbie still hesitated. "I've never been to the White Hussar. You're certain you prefer that, sir?"

"Yes," Mr. Rennie said briefly. "Now buzz."

And as Refrigeration United summoned the waiter, Mrs. Debrett was dreamily marveling: "Here I am, already involved with two complete strangers, and about to meet a third! What next?"

A red velvet jewel box of a supper-club was the answer, with the White Hussar skating across the glass lid of the entrance hall. No merry holly berries here, nor come-hither mistletoe, but clusters of Christmas roses, exquisite but aloof in little glass alcoves. Specimens enshrined! It was all as refined as the angel. Here was no babble but a leisurely hush. Soft music and silent service, with ample space—each table a sparkling island mirrored on the dance floor.

"This is going to cost the earth," Mrs. Debrett decided, for

Mr. Rennie had been received as reverently as a crowned head. "But probably he's a shareholder. Anyway, Bess is in luck!"

And there Bess was, in black! Beside her tall brother, small and dark, but quietly well aware. Strictly speaking, the Christmas angel was not beautiful. Graceful, yes, and at a glance Mrs. Debrett divined a dress sense that had saved the girl from the commonplace of the present period. The black two-piece was as cleverly tailored as a riding-habit. It had distinction. The gray-eyed Bess suggested a romantic young widow of nineteen.

As the little party shook hands, another thought secretly surprised them all: *But we know each other . . . this has happened before . . . how very strange!*

Aloud, they merely smiled and nodded in reassurance. There was plenty of time for everything. The rest of their lives, in fact.

Mr. Rennie's table, raised two steps above the floor, in its vermilion recess, left them enthroned. Bess's face was faintly flushed now—supper had been delectable . . . and the music wheedled.

"Young lady," her host inquired, "don't you want to dance?"

The Christmas angel shook her head. "No, thank you very much. I've got rubbers on my soles. Besides, it's more than enough to watch. . . . Just look at that gorgeous girl dancing cheek to cheek—"

"Quiet, Bess!" Robert was glaring. "She's the girl I told you about." His friends felt paradise tremble.

"Robbie!" the gorgeous girl in a rose-patterned frock had turned, astounded. Skimming away from her partner, "In all this world," she cried, "how wonderful!"

But Mrs. Debrett was too quick for her. "Princess Lointoine," ceremoniously she addressed Bess, "may we present Miss Sandra Jevons?"

Both men had risen, as the Princesse bowed with a certain reserve.

"*Enchantée,*" she murmured, then motioned her suite to be seated.

With a gasp the earlier angel exclaimed: "Such a surprise —I never dreamed . . ." her confusion almost suggested nightmare. "Well, I must fly!" And for once she moved with the speed of light.

But Robert, startled, had his eye on Mrs. Debrett. That lady was still smiling. That anyone of her age should be such a dazzler! Only the young, he had imagined, could be so alive.

Later, when bidding goodby, "Thank you for everything," he said, and added soberly: "I wouldn't have missed tonight for the world."

Along the wet pavement the young people walked away. No taxi was needed, for, as they explained, the rain had stopped, and, anyway, Bess had rubbers on her shoes.

"And we who have outlived our hearts," Mr. Rennie inquired, "what happens to us now? May I drive you home? For, of course, I know as well as if I held it in my hand that you have never had a rubber on your sole."

Complacently Mrs. Debrett replied: "I am insulated in other ways. Certainly you may drive me back—though I realize that you have been a demon in your day."

Mr. Rennie glanced at his watch. "And *that* is just beginning." In the mysterious light of the street lamp, he added quietly, "Happy Christmas, angel!"

The Mask

The Mask

A clumsy face, a strange face, no, an ugly face, decided the short-sighted old gentleman from his unusual seat in a suburban carriage. Painful, in fact. A pity that he had put down his paper.

Then, as the train still hung fire on Hungerford Bridge, he stole another glance, repelled and yet oddly fascinated, for it was impossible to guess the man's age. Quite well dressed, though. The figure was that of a well-set young man. The hair was vigorous, the hands energetic, sensitive. Might have been those of a doctor, or a surgeon, if it hadn't been for that face. Enough to frighten the French, as his old grandmother used to say.

The young man turned and the observer saw him full face. What a mistake he'd made! Not a clumsy, strange, or ugly face—this was no botched job of nature, but a triumph of surgical skill. A new face. An ageless mask. The incredible feat. Achievement.

The old gentleman's breath quickened. He had caught a glance from the mask's eyes—cold, gray, observant eyes. Every other face in the carriage was still hidden by the morning paper. He alone was trapped.

"Looks as if it might clear," he said instantly but too brightly.

"Morning mist," said the mask briefly.

As the old gentleman regained the pleasant anonymity of the platform, the welcome width of Charing Cross, he drew back for a second in the pell-mell stream of passengers that blotted out the other. With a truant sense of guilt the words from Goldsmith's *The Deserted Village* convicted him again: "Well had the boding tremblers learned to trace the day's disasters in his morning face."

But ahead of the queue, and as usual abreast of time, the Mask strode on across Trafalgar Square, and spanked up Haymarket. He had decided against a bus. For once he'd let up and do as he pleased. Kirby-Wright had advised him not to force things. That old boy in the train, domed head, guileless blue eye, safely sleeping the last years away—routed by consternation. Too bad! No, he couldn't *face* the bus today. Hell—that pun again!

October sunshine, mild, shadowless, had dispersed the earlier haze. The windless day, and streets still empty held something of the sequestered charm of an earlier era. He might, after all, have been a figure in some old print, introduced to give scale, instead of one of the Guardian Insurance Company's valuers unsuitably hastening, neck and neck, to beat the office boy in achieving sanctuary first.

Neck and neck—Kirby-Wright said those assinine associations sped through every mind, but were ignored. Let them pass. His business was to dwell on the essential.

Abruptly he stopped outside Ashlar's window in Dover Street. The stillness of this plate glass shrine was freshly hung with Pomona-green velvet, framing a solitary Kang-he porcelain, peerless in beauty. In the level morning beam the vase appeared to ripen visibly. On the Imperial yellow ground, panels in *famille verte* disclosed the ancient pine tree, cloud, and rock with the severity of the Chinese classical period.

Enchanted he stared and automatically computed: Four thousand. Might fetch more, even today. But Ashlar did not specialize in Oriental china. This would set the heather on fire in Bond Street!

Enlivened he moved on, his pace now normal. He'd look into this at luncheon.

But he did not. By luncheon time dynamic events had overtaken him.

This morning, to his astonishment, the Managing Director had outstripped both office boy and himself, was even now awaiting him with the startling news that Mr. Cardiff had died in the night. He could hardly credit it—Cardiff, an active fifty, irascible with energy! Clients at first prejudiced by his gruffness were finally impressed by the probity which so starkly declared him; this although most were quite incapable of assessing his unique ability. He had recently become a director. It was impossible that he should be dead. Upon his verdicts hung the day. Hang it all, he *was* the Guardian!

At eleven o'clock the Managing Director again sent for him.

"Now, Scott, this situation must be dealt with at once. Hope there's going to be no nonsense! We can't have you sitting here like a broody hen much longer. You're a much younger man than Cardiff but no one else in the firm today has had your training or experience. The Chairman will be here by one o'clock. The Board intend you to carry on in Cardiff's place."

Clients' houses; dealers' showrooms; buyers' offices at home and abroad; other people's faces—an unending procession of consternation or aversion fleetly concealed.

Obdurately he declared: "I tell you again, I affect people. It prejudices business. I ought to remain at the office end."

"Rubbish! You're not a shopwalker. You exaggerate the thing. You suffer more than most people who see you because you're—well, sensitive to appearances. Anyway, the Board's no longer prepared to have you coquetting with clients behind that glass screen. Your work's in the open. If you can't have courage, have common sense. This is promotion. And as a start you'll have to leave on Friday for Wiltshire. That assessment on Lord Hurleigh's library. Damage from water. Diverse items. Furniture as well as folios. Just up your street! The reservations will be at Mindon Manor Hotel for the week end. Take your wife with you. Change will do you good. That's final."

This is promotion! The crowded evening train jolted and jostled him back along its corridor to the same peremptory tune.

If you can't have courage, have common sense! Damn *cheek,* he decided violently, but only paid the pun a flying admission in the pressure of present dismay.

Yet as he opened the garden gate perturbation, as always, fell away. The small, embowered house, a wedding gift from his wife's parents, stood back from the leafy road in the green, rustling twilight of its own garden. At that bewitching moment of dusk, before immediate dark, when roof, chimney, tree top disengage from shadows as if the absent light still molded them, each was sealed from trespass in its own domain, lending diversity to a solitude that was one in loveliness as well as loneliness.

He drew a deep breath of satisfaction.

"Joyce!"

"Darling!"

Each night they met with the fervor of those who have been parted for years, or by some major misfortune—the day's decline blindly, wildly repaired in that convulsive embrace.

"This *is* promotion!" sagely she affirmed it, seated in the lamplight, after supper. As pretty as a posy she was stitching linen buttons with a briskness that belied dark, pensive eyes. And with the immemorial hauteur of all wives she added: "At last they realize that they can't get on without you—that you *are* the business. High time too!"

Supinely he grunted, as he opened his book which he always read with one fine hand shielding his eyes—between them. It was the best moment of their day, until upstairs, when the light was out and they lay safe in the darkness, one with earlier memory. Mrs. Scott was not a reader and tonight she interrupted recklessly.

"The Buxtons once motored Mummy to Mindon Manor for lunch. She said it was terrific. Waiters in white gloves and nothing the slightest trouble. Too marvelous! We'll have to take your dinner jacket and my rose evening dress. But for safety the first night I'll wear my best afternoon frock until we see what the others look like. It will be wonderful, but—"

"But what?" he said cheerfully.

"We're so happy here. And at the week ends popping into this little roadhouse or that. Just our two selves. *Must* we go?"

"Of course we must," he said evenly. "Now, don't get het up on my account. Sooner or later we have to push out. No one will patronize me with sympathy once they've seen my beautiful spouse—a face that launched a thousand surgeons—ships, I mean."

Adroitly she said, "Aunt Helen would have been at home there."

Aunt Helen who had brought him up. And on a pittance,

too. Aunt Helen who used to boast: "Born with a silver spoon in his mouth—Georgian at that!" That had been long before the war, when he was still blessed with luck and looks as well as outstanding ability. In the days when everyone had thought he was too good for Joyce. Joyce had thought this also. People always looked twice at him, even in the street, but he was the happy warrior, a man fascinated by his work, his half-shy, half sceptical attitude to women that of the handsome male as yet unspoiled. His perfunctory attitude to romance had made his whirlwind courtship more of a miracle still. Joyce had been spellbound by bliss.

During the engagement the crash had come.

Everyone said it was the end. Joyce's critics had been foremost in agreement that no girl could be expected—

But precisely then Joyce had come into her own. Yet what a struggle it had been with relations, friends, above all with him, himself! Her parents had not then learned to accept the inevitable —that he was hers, and hers alone! That blurred mask, in agonizing contrast with its original, yet enabled her to recognize him as strangers could not do. There were clues. To her he was now as familiar as a face seen in a fog—a fog of flesh. And to him, she was the only woman in the world—a world of two.

In this fight to a finish for her marriage, Dr. Kirby-Wright, astonishingly, had come out on her side.

Yet alone at that private interview, she had not known at first how the day would go. Dr. Kirby-Wright had asked her some curious questions that had nothing to do with surgery. As always, in extremity, she had responded with simplicity, and been carried beyond her depth. Her face was pale with intensity as she answered his questions. Everything hung on this man and she knew it.

"Are you an only child, like your fiancé?" he asked finally.

"Yes," she said, and it seemed to her that he hesitated.

"Does it matter?" she ventured.

For the first time he smiled. "It makes a difference. You will both have the august rather than the democratic approach, but you will at least understand each other. I am inclined to think that this compensates for much."

He rose as he spoke. "I have to be a little careful, you see. This amounts to taking you into partnership with me. You will have to finish my job. I can't do that. Perhaps only one woman in a hundred can. I think," he gave her another glance from a cold blue eye, "that you may be successful."

She, the unlikely, the unsuitable, had left his consulting room with the tremulous certainty that she had been decorated. Her admiration for Dr. Kirby-Wright was become veneration. She felt dedicated—or committed, which was it?

A week after marriage, this query slyly imposed itself.

Seated just as they were now, he had opened his book for the first time, and for the first time raised his hand to shade his eyes.

Breathlessly, she realized that it was just as if calamity had not been.

"What beautiful hands you have," she said softly. Then her heart galloped with guilt. She could feel again the cold appraisal of Dr. Kirby-Wright.

"Sweet child," said her husband quietly, in that deep, resonant voice that always thrilled her, but obligingly he did not stir. Her charm had worked.

Biting her lip, then as now, she began to sew.

Silence settled upon the comfortable but tastelessly furnished room. Most of its contents had come to the young people through the kindness of her parents, but an old print on the wall, a Sheraton cabinet in the corner and a faded fire screen mutely gave evidence of another sort of elegance in a losing battle with plump unholstery, glossy veneers, and art silk curtains. There had been talk at the start of a satinwood dining room suite, but he had fought with ferocity against this benefaction.

He loathed her shell-pink bedroom color scheme. Eagerly she confided: "I want the bathroom to match—bath, basin, throne, everything! Then it will feel like a suite, won't it?"

He had resisted a temptation to laugh, but a feeling of hopelessness had invaded him. These interior decorations, which had emerged from the hands of a local firm, shrimp rather than shell-pink, afflicted him as much as did the modern Nativity in sentimental blues and greens which she had hung above the bedroom mantelpiece. They were as much a bloomer as the vase of flowers on the piano. Yet Joyce was musical. She played rather well. He could not broach the subject as it was surely self-evident that a piano was a musical instrument, and that the vase upon it was as absurd as a bow upon a bookcase. She was sublimely unaware. Sublimely was the word. And yet how petty to criticize when there she sat, as pretty, as appealing as a child, as ardent as a goddess, as mild as a mother. The perfect wife—and he, of all people!

He glanced up. The clock was striking ten but what he suddenly saw was a small Italian casket which he had picked up at a sale—a valuable find—and which once again she had set out at an angle on the mantelpiece, as if it were coquetting with the china cat she kept for luck.

As they rose to go upstairs, automatically he altered the line of the box, and, for the first time, lightly said: "This should stand four-square with the wall."

"Oh, *no!*" she protested. "Ornaments should *always* be at angles."

"Couldn't *we* start an innovation?" he asked, pleasantly.

"Of course," she gave an uncertain little laugh, as they stood beside the dying fire. "Such a trifle."

But as she left the room behind him, absently she again altered the position of the box.

Yet Mindon Manor on Friday night found them hand-fasted as one beneath the dinner table, while gazing sternly around them at the decorous damask, glittering glass, and the towering but subdued splendor of claret velvet curtains.

"Honeymooners," affirmed their waiter. " 'Orrible, poor fellow! Don't know which I'm sorriest for."

"Give them the *petits-fours* off the à la carte," said the headwaiter. "You can add the *sorbet* too. That girl's a heroine."

The stately eighteenth-century room appeared to be festooned in silence. The other guests seated themselves soundlessly, with an amiability that was dreamlike in its quietude. The gala of laughter, the gaiety of voices, the tinkling of ice in an ice bucket, the popping of a cork were here agreeably muted—elfin echoes pleasurably haunting a well-bred hush.

From the corner of her mouth she intoned: "This *is* promotion!" a dry little aside characteristic of her when overwhelmed. He loved this trait in her—the ability to poke fun at herself on occasion. Their eyes met.

His eyes were all right. She used to drown herself in his eyes, her face transformed by love. There a wordless communion took place. Their spirits were here revealed, clear but isolated, like life seen through a telescope. This was sanctuary. But any passing shadow herein amounted to eclipse.

Three people seated themselves at the next table.

A tall soldierly man with a white cavalry mustache; an

elegant woman of thirty accompanied by a dark, distinguished husband. These three persons were of unusual height and compelling dignity. Benignly they regarded the young couple, and later that night, when they left the lounge, the three bowed a courteous goodnight.

With a sense of exhilaration the Scotts regained their luxurious bedroom.

Next morning, in the writing room, the first words were spoken.

The elegant Mrs. Temperley borrowed some envelopes from Joyce's table, and said how pleasant she found it to relax for once on a Saturday morning. Impossible as it was to picture Mrs. Temperley in anything as pedestrian as a queue, Joyce swiftly agreed. Then in the most natural way it transpired that Mrs. Scott's husband was still at work—on Lord Hurleigh's treasures across the park.

"Fascinating!" declared Mrs. Temperley. "The insight, as well as the experience, needed for such a career leaves the rest of us humbled. My husband would value his opinion of the brasses in the village church here. Perhaps you would join us for coffee after luncheon? My father, General Grier, as an old soldier, will also be delighted to meet him."

The girl's face flushed. "My husband didn't have any wartime experiences, as such," she said hurriedly. "He got his packet, as he calls it, the first day out."

People always wondered what compensation he'd got, apart from his pension, and in her exasperation she'd got into the habit of forestalling sharply, as she did now. "No decorations—wounds only."

Today for the first time the pathos, the perfection of this reply struck her, so gravely beneficent was the look bent upon her by Mrs. Temperley. "My dear child," she said softly, "there is a valor for which no V.C. suffices. It calls for a living decoration, which he has in you."

Never before had Joyce's devotion been so gracefully acknowledged. A sense of poise and pleasure secretly, sweetly informed her, and the coffee party was a signal success. By the time the neighboring brasses had been visited, the Guardian Insurance Company's chief valuer had come triumphantly into his own. Proudly his wife listened, for there appeared to be no end to this authoritative knowledge of his. And through it she was happily aware of General Grier's hearty, and Professor Temperley's quizzical, approval of her own quiet, pretty self. Indeed both men formed a kind of bodyguard for her, when next day Mrs. Temperley again tirelessly plied Mr. Scott with queries that were as readily answered.

In the spate of conversation that now flowed round and from Mr. Scott, his tragic appearance was almost forgotten. Joyce had never heard a talker like Mrs. Temperley. Neither the General nor Professor Temperley could keep up with her. It was a miracle that her own husband could!

Now Mrs. Temperley was talking of someone called Rilke. Joyce did not know the name, but surprisingly enough, her husband did.

Suddenly the young wife stiffened. It was not a person they were talking about. It was poetry, and her husband was leaning forward, with enthusiasm in his pleasant voice.

"Poetry's my blind spot," the General was admitting to pretty little Mrs. Scott, "but very much my daughter's line of country. She's even had some published."

Politely Mrs. Scott smiled as, stunned, she watched her husband vanishing into this unknown territory with Mrs. Temperley. Kierkegaard was the next name she caught. Had Mr. Scott read much of Kierkegaard? Mr. Scott had read nothing. But Mr.

Scott *must!* Mrs. Temperley would send Kierkegaard. Kierkegaard was a revelation, for Kierkegaard had pointed out that although one could not proceed from doubt, one *could* proceed from despair.

Genially Mr. Scott nodded. "He's certainly got something there!" And even the General finally deserted Mrs. Scott on a laugh, "Nothing like bedrock for a foundation—ha, ha!"

Rigid now in her chair, she had not the faintest idea of what they meant. Talking for talking's sake, she told herself resentfully. Smart-set stuff, that was about it!

Worse was to follow. Professor Temperley related next a curious experience that he and his wife had recently had—in which disclosure had sprung quite simply from bedrock of another sort. Secretly the caretaker at their block had used the Temperley's flat to entertain his friends, while they were on holiday. "We have rather a fine radio," the Professor smiled. "But my wife tumbled to the fact that the premises were being used by a small but telling detail! All was immaculate on our return, but cushions, chairs, and ornaments had each been replaced at the angle dear to the uneducated eye."

Two bright roses flamed in Mrs. Scott's pale face, and the terrible, the incredible thing was that her husband was laughing heartily, as if he'd noticed nothing. Merciful as this was, obscurely she knew it to be unforgivable. In angry confusion, a panic of insecurity, she could hardly sit the last hour out, and on their way upstairs alone, passionately she turned:

"Oh, darling, I can't bear it. Let's go home tomorrow."

"Home?" his amazement was complete. "I thought you were enjoying every minute. So you said. Only this afternoon."

Miserably she turned away. "Perhaps I'm homesick."

"That's absurd—when I'm here! In any case, we can't. I've still got a full day's work on that library tomorrow."

By six o'clock on Monday night, Mrs. Scott had such a splitting headache that she could not face the dining room.

A remorseful husband tendered explanations downstairs, before seating himself in solitary state to dine.

A delightful little meal was sent upstairs. She picked at it with a pounding heart. This would be the test. Would he come upstairs or would he linger?

He came at once.

Closely on his heels, a waiter followed with flowers from the General, fruit from Professor and Mrs. Temperley, and sympathy from all! Mrs. Scott was once more center stage. Peacefully peeling a peach, in her pastel pink bed jacket, she looked and felt a dream.

At an appropriately early hour, an adoring husband turned out their light.

"My headache has gone," she whispered accommodatingly.

In the dark he answered: "Clever puss!" which somewhat startled her. At such moments "Beloved child" was his usual endearment.

She lay awake later with a ludicrous sense of loss.

Clever puss—this would never do!

Something had happened, but what?

Chastened, she found herself clinging tenaciously to the tangible. Unlike that caretaker, she could learn. As soon as she got home—

Home proved sheer perfection. Thankfully she found it enclosed them both again. There was nothing to change here.

Then followed the first and fatal dinner at the Temperley's flat. Their home was not nearly as grand as she expected. Scarcely grand at all. Sparse, she called it, the walnut furniture bleached with age, the color scheme so subdued as to look shabby. A few dark paintings on the walls, and not a flower in the drawing room, only some Venetian glass winking and blinking against the light, as brilliant but as brittle as Mrs. Temperley herself. Yet there was Joyce's husband exclaiming at this and that, he who had barely said he liked his own beautiful home the first time he'd seen it!

Well, if this were what he wanted . . .

Next day, compressing her lips, she had walked round the house, altering each arrangement and removing certain things he had criticized.

Finally she could have wept—at this, her own sanctuary, which had also changed its face subject to some relentless decree. But she must keep his adoration at all costs, even the cost of her own comfort.

Pausing in the middle of a much emptier room, a happier thought occurred to her: Perhaps he would not notice any difference after all?

But he did—immediately.

Her voice sharpened as she said: "You think it is an improvement?"

"Improvement—I should think so! This is something like the thing!" His enthusiasm was an offense.

During the months that followed, she settled down to her resentment.

In business his progress privately left her breathless. Every week saw alterations in plans. Change of address for professional reasons was now only a matter of time. Already the mystic circle of a world of two had enlarged alarmingly with the Temperleys' numerous introductions. She now found herself panting behind a wholly adequate husband in this advance upon the heights. It was as if the mask, the symbol of his suffering and her sacrifice, had been dealt with once and for all at Mindon Manor. In fact, his present robust attitude appeared to have allotted an exchange of parts in the same play, as more and more she was obliged to withdraw behind a martyred brow. His chief crime, a total inability to realize that the Temperley intrusion was at the bottom of this misery, exacted its own penalty. Surprising little quarrels flared up weekly now. Invariably over trifles. In major matters she faithfully followed his lead. There was no real fault to be found in her. And he was at a loss to account for his increasing discomfort at home—her erratic ire. Their garden lounge on these early summer evenings, gilded by the setting sun had become for him the expression of his mixed fortunes: a golden horizon, but their roof tree disappearing into the darkness of its own zenith.

Unexpectedly he canceled a Sunday luncheon at the Temperleys to fulfill a business appointment in Holland, taking his wife with him.

Her happiness was ecstatic, her face propitious as a May morning. Uneasily he basked in this unusual blandness.

At Amsterdam it ceased abruptly during a brief visit to the Ryksmuseum. Certain pictures aroused her disapproval. This she voiced so explicitly that he felt embarrassment. People, close by in the gallery, moved away from them. She might have been expressing a personal antagonism, so rancorous was her criticism.

In Amsterdam, too, as she followed him round the Stadmuseum, crisis occurred. The Van Gogh pictures gave rise to exclamations of such ridicule that brusquely he turned upon her.

"Please lower your voice. Other people speak English. You are giving offense."

"But I never saw such daubs! And supposed to be masterpieces. What impudence getting away with stuff like that!" She laughed more shrilly than she had intended, and he took her elbow, and steered her out of the gallery.

"Look here, Joyce," he said, "I don't know if I am the bitterness you're suffering from or not, but I suggest you nurse it elsewhere. I'm taking you back to the hotel now, as I mean to see those pictures in peace."

Her heart sank in a sickening way at the gulf set by his words. This wasn't a quarrel. It was far worse—a separation, and as she didn't know its element of distance, she could not bridge it.

Yet fleetly she said: "Silly boy to fuss. I won't say another word. But of course I must go round with you. It's what I've come for, after all. To learn."

But beneath her placating silence which for the rest of the day gently wooed him, the foundations trembled. A revolution was in progress. The tyrant in her was dismayed. On all sides she could feel this threat of earthquake, for she was further oppressed by the cosmopolitan splendor of the hotel and its impressive staff. Her husband, quelling those omnipresent waiters with brevity and dignity, had become a stranger to her. His face—his face was just the same, yet people did not seem to notice his affliction as they had done. She had become the odd man out.

"I've lost him, I've lost him," she realized. "It's hideous."

Averting her eyes from her own image in the hotel mirror, she recognized that *her* face was changing. No good blaming the rich food or the central heating for ruining her complexion, she decided. She looked a wreck because she was a wreck. The dear little roadhouses, the country inns where she had queened it, were gone forever, with his ideal of her, his adoration. And without that she could not live.

That night, observing her marked pallor, he relented sufficiently to say: "Forget today! You're musical, Joyce, you'd never pass judgment on a song or a symphony till you'd heard it out. Well, a picture takes time too. Try to see it out."

Her mouth trembled as she said: "Forgive me. I haven't been myself for months. I'm going to have a baby."

Pride had delayed this announcement until certainty could vouch for her.

"My darling child!" he said.

In sixty seconds she had regained her foothold.

There was nothing she could not, would not bear now in gratitude!

But guilt had dug its own ditch, another kind of channel, and through this grave she had to pass, her only right of way.

At home fresh invitations from the Temperleys, further books, but meekly Mrs. Scott sewed on at nights.

Nothing had altered, after all, except that, terrified, she now sewed sweetly.

Sometimes she detected a teasing note in her husband's voice. Was her amiability overdone? Was her sweetness become sickly? Steadfastly she ignored this, his darling child.

A graver consideration was making its weight felt—*our darling child.*

Little doubts, small suspicions, growing fears about herself flocked on her as her time drew near. Old wives' tales, odd stories she had heard reared their bogey heads. Frantically she reminded herself that nothing could touch their child. It was heredity that counted. Her husband's face, the result of calamity, was an outside occurrence. But there remained the whispered tales of strange sights seen by mothers, and children later born imperfect. Panic-stricken she found herself dwelling on the thought, the escape of a miscarriage—only to reject this with still wilder aversion.

Yet throughout this phantom invasion she maintained a stoic silence. True to her own autocracy, in her world of one, her remaining sanity seemed to be invested in this reserve. Moreover, how could other people deal with these intangibles? Above all, she was ashamed to have her own rout declared, so peculiarly her own did it seem.

After herculean struggles by day, she slept soundly at night. There is a limit, she decided dully. Her husband, astonished at the indifference she showed to bodily discomfort, was unaware that this could be discounted after such spectral battling.

Seated beside him at night, he seemed to her remote as a better land, as unobtainable as heaven. "Why," she thought, surprised, "he is the passion of my life."

For a moment she had the rewarding sense of another sphere in which this irresistible creature maintained his dominion invisibly, infallibly.

She stole a glance at him. As the mysterious power behind that mask, he now awoke a sense of reverence in her. "At any rate, I love him," she concluded. "If it isn't all that matters, it is enough."

In a curious way she arose from this one-sided meal restored as never before.

Did other wives, she wondered naively, feel such consuming passion for their husbands? And her imagination was quickened by the richness, the complexity of this unusual idea. Faint but far-off in her world of one, she had caught a cheering echo— the mustering horn of fellowship.

Next day as she dusted it, she opened for the first time, the book he had last been reading.

Poetry by someone called Sassoon. The pages parted of their own accord at a place that he had marked. Lines he had liked. She frowned. Poetry had always been beyond her.

None are exempt from service in this hour;
And vanquished in ourselves we dare not be.

That was quite plain. She could follow that. Her surprise became elation. She read on:

Now for a sunlit future, we can show
The clenched resolve, endurance that defies
Daemons in dark—and toward that future go
With earth's defended freedom in our eyes.

Trembling with wonder she sat down in her husband's chair. *Daemons in dark* . . . it was the most amazing thing she'd ever known! *With earth's defended freedom in our eyes.* That was what it meant then? Why it was tremendous.

Her husband had been through terrible things. They had always been an exceptional couple, but that was not the staggering thing about this revelation. The Poet was the amazing thing, the Poet who had written these words! He too had known. Was the whole world full of people suffering like this?

On that instant, a compassion fearless because informed swept her beyond harbor, breasting unimagined seas of sorrow. But seas not solitary. In that lay salvation. She had slipped her cable. She was launched at last, one in a world of many. Free. And as the elements know their own, when least she had expected it, she found herself supported . . . sailing in an expanding universe where the daemons sangs like angels.

Their child was one month old on another winter evening when crisply she said: "There's quite a good shade on that lamp, dear—take your hand down."

Comfortably he obeyed, without glancing from his book until the child she was nursing stirred.

Perfect in every particular, she noted, with the calm of

(37

aftermath. He was her secret, and what he had cost her, yet there he lay as snug and smug as a daisy!

Infatuated they gazed at it. The husband's blank face bent closer, as he watched the domed brow of a future sage, the guileless blue eyes drowsing the first years away! Suddenly these eyes opened. A gleam of satisfaction wrinkled the infant's face. With delight, he smiled into the mask.

The husband was the first to recover.

"I can see," he said, dryly, "that this fellow has put my nose out of joint."

Merrily she agreed.

They had forgotten the mask. They had achieved that miracle for them—a normal attitude. It was not courage, it was not common sense. It was promotion.

Third Class to Joy

Third Class to Joy

It was Christmas Eve. As Robert Munn ran down the station road he saw that the last train to Glasgow was already at the platform. His small suitcase and the empty attaché case that had once held his traveling samples bumped against his short, stockily built body. Why run, he thought indignantly, to catch a train that could only take him to a dead end? Nevertheless, he continued to run because he was a methodical, conscientious man, and quite apart from the anger welling up within him against the world in general and his brother in particular, he was annoyed with himself for cutting the time so fine. Fortunately he had his return ticket.

Pushing past the collector, he saw the train shunt back and dashed at the third-class corridor carriage nearest him. A young girl stood on the platform saying goodby to a solitary traveler inside. He elbowed her aside, opened the door and climbed in. He was breathing hard, and his eyes were bloodshot. He looked forty-five, instead of the thirty-five years of his age.

(41

"Goodby, uncle," cried the girl. "I'm so glad they're meeting you. A happy Christmas, darling."

Mechanically Munn noted the words as he thrust his cases onto the rack, then sank down, closing his eyes.

The train moved out. *A happy Christmas!* With maddening insistence the wheels ground this irony into his soul. *A happy Christmas!* All his life he had borne burdens. And now this last was insupportable. But why should he stand it? Why live through tomorrow, Christmas day, to take up a twopenny-halfpenny job the next morning? Why begin the struggle again and from the foot of the ladder this time? No, he couldn't go through with it. He would make an end of things tonight. There was always the river. Nobody cared a tinker's curse for him in any case. And any way he'd miss Christmas day, alone in that commercial hotel, listening to other leftovers, like himself, getting drunk. He himself had never been able to drink.

Involuntarily he groaned aloud.

"Can I do anything for you?" said a deep, singularly pleasant voice beside him.

Munn opened his eyes. And having opened them, stared, for the man opposite was regarding him with a compassion that bereft Munn temporarily of words.

"No!" he replied shortly. "I'm just a bit sick, that's all."

"I'm sorry," said his companion. "I realize I am, possibly, intruding, but if I could be of help—"

"No one can."

"Is it as bad as that?"

"Worse!" Munn said briefly, and then in spite of himself swallowed his confusion. Never before had he looked into such a sympathetic face. And some words that his mother used to quote came back to him, something about the seeing eye and understanding heart. No great harm telling the fellow a bit about it.

After all he'd never see him again, for he could spot at a glance the chap was a cut above him. "Tonight for the first time in my life I've had to ask for a loan. It's been the last straw."

"I see!" said the other gently, so gently that Munn interrupted.

"No, you don't. Instead he gave me advice. What d'you think of that?"

"Advice under those circumstances," said his companion promptly, "is outrageous."

"That's what I've been saying ever since," said Munn, a trifle less angrily. "Outrageous!"

"He is your brother, possibly?"

"He's my brother all right. It's outrageous!" The word seemed to appease him.

"And probably you've done a good deal for him?"

"Well, I set them all on their feet. But then I was the eldest. It was only natural. Yet now when I ask for a couple of hundred, it's 'Sorry, I would if I could but I can't.' You know. The usual. Of course I can manage without it." The other nodded attentively. "I can always manage. But if I'd had it to put into the job that I'm taking up the day after tomorrow, it would have made a big difference to my position with these new people. You see, it's like this . . ." and before he knew what he was doing, disarmed by the mild and listening stranger, Munn was telling the story of how he'd built up Munn's Enduring Belts and Braces, only to lose the business through no fault of his own—"and I paid up every penny, more fool me!" But he made no mention of Jenny's faithlessness, nor all that the divorce had cost him. "That's the long and the short of it," he wound up aggressively. "And now it's back to the beginning for yours truly. Not much to hang on for under those circumstances."

"Except," and his listener spoke with a certain authority,

"that with your past experience, you will probably now prove invincible."

"Invincible?"

"Yes, Mr. ——?" began the other.

"Munn's the name."

"Yes, Mr. Munn, invincible, for you are a virtuous man, are you not?"

"Virtuous?" Munn started. He found the Biblical flavor of the word, as applied to himself, faintly shocking. "I've always been the clean potato, if that's what you mean."

"Exactly—a man of good will!" the stranger nodded. "Life can have little more to teach you, Mr. Munn. I feel confident that the worst is over. Yes, the reward is on its way."

"The *reward?*"

"Peace. And high time for it too—the very season! Peace and goodwill!" And now not even the dreary light of the railway carriage could defeat the peculiar animation streaming from this traveler's face. There was a feeling of health about the man that was contagious.

"Peace and goodwill," Munn mumbled awkwardly. "You look as if you knew a thing or two about those!"

"Yes," agreed the other smiling. "One day I awoke to the fact that continual suffering was a fruitless experience. So I decided to tune in to joy. Of course it took a little time to—to master the new technique. But eventually I succeeded."

"You must be cracked."

"On the contrary, I now am whole—" The amusement in the stranger's voice was replaced by a greater earnestness. "Mr. Munn, I wonder if you will do me a favor? Will you give me a Christmas present?"

"A *present?*" Munn found himself stuttering.

"Yes."

Again Munn stared at him, nonplussed. "All right, fire ahead. What sort do you want?"

The other looked down modestly. "It is rather expensive I'm afraid. Half a minute of your time last thing every night and first thing every morning for six days. Just as you are falling asleep I would like you to say these words for me: *'Third Class to Joy!'*"

"Honest to goodness, you're balmy!" exclaimed Munn. "I suppose this has something to do with your technique as you call it. Well, let me tell you this: If there was anything in it we'd all be in heaven by this time! Come on now, admit it! If it does the trick, as you say it did with you, why doesn't everyone do it?"

"Because it's so difficult."

"Difficult to spout those four words for thirty seconds last thing at night, first thing in the morning, for six days?"

"And preserve this continuity for that time—Yes, the hardest thing in the world. Not one person in a thousand has the requisite strength of character for this. You may prefer the word concentration."

"Well, look here," interrupted Munn, "I'm not one in a thousand. But I'm not the sort to be stumped by a fiddling little thing like that. I could manage it easy as winking if I set my mind to it. *Third Class to Joy!* I never heard such stuff!"

"In a month or two you might manage it," agreed the other pleasantly, "but to get the six days in order from the start—Impossible!"

"I tell you I can do it in a week. Any mutt might!"

"Mr. Munn, a new world in a week has only happened once before in history!"

"Look here—"

"But at any rate I see that I can count on my present!"

"Oh, I'll do it all right. *Third Class to Joy.* It doesn't

mean a thing to me. But I'll do it in a week. That's to say if I don't forget to start tonight."

"I'm afraid," said the other, and again his eyelids drooped apologetically, "that you will not forget, at any rate not for a time."

Munn's answer died uneasily. Who on earth was the man? There was something about him that set him apart. The girl on the platform had called him "uncle." That was ordinary enough. Munn was an uncle himself.

The train ground over the points. In a minute or two they would arrive. Munn lifted his cases down. He could feel that the other was watching him with a smile. Dash it all, he would miss the fellow! But he wasn't going to suggest another meeting. Although Robert Munn was as good as the next fellow, he'd be the last to push himself in where he didn't belong. "I don't mind admitting," he turned and looked down at the stranger, "that I feel a sight better than I did when I got into the train. Thanks for your company."

"I too have enjoyed our talk, Mr. Munn. I have rather a sensitive ear, and you have, if I may say so, a very harmonious voice."

"You're a musician, maybe?"

"Unfortunately, no. But I am an artist of sorts. I have always been interested in painting."

"Pictures?"

"Pictures."

There was a pause. They were running into Central Station. The dark buildings of Eglinton Street towered beside them.

"Do you know Glasgow well, Mr. Munn?"

"Like the back of my hand. I was born here. Could find my way about in my sleep."

"I can see that you have a feeling for the place. No doubt you have some special haunts?"

"Don't know about haunts, but I often drop in to Craig's in Gordon Street about eleven for a cup of coffee. I spend ten minutes. Neither more nor less. The waitress knows to bring the check with the coffee."

"As I imagined—a man of resolution."

"Resolution your foot!" said Munn good naturedly. "Habit's my other name. That's why you'll probably get your blessed present." As the train slid into the station, he added: "You're being met, aren't you?"

But the stranger did not answer. Instead he held out his hand. "Christmas is almost upon us, my friend. I'm not going to wish you a happy one. You deserve more than that. I wish you the joyful New Year that is already yours."

For the first time a smile flickered across Munn's face, making it look oddly young, in a woebegone way. "At it again, Mr. Joy!" he said. "It's clear to me that Habit's your second name too. But thanks all the same."

"And now," said the stranger almost diffidently, "as you have luggage, I wonder if you would be kind enough to step out first—"

"Rather," interrupted Munn, "and get you a porter?"

"No," said the stranger reluctantly, "I do not require a porter. I must wait here until I am collected. You see—I am blind."

*Greetings
from Gwennie*

Greetings from Gwennie

A memorable, a unique occasion! From the balcony of the town hall the mayor, flanked by trumpeters proclaimed to the multitude of May 7, 1910: "George . . . by the Grace of God!"

At that instant Mr. George Rennie caught a jocular flash from his wife's ice-blue eye, and the inspiring, almost heroic affinity of his Christian name with the king's died at birth. Rhoda was the arch-debunker.

It was the same derisive gaiety that had first struck like lightning with Gwennie's Christmas card.

"Don't be silly, George. You must remember who she was—or rather is. The very fact that she doesn't put her second name shows you knew her—know her well."

"I tell you, Rhoda, that there were two, perhaps three girls called Gwen, who turned up at the Boughton balls. I can't remember which it was, or might be."

"But this is Gwennie, George. There is an intimacy about Gwennie!"

Ludicrous that his marriage had, for five years now, taken an undoubted turn for the worse on the strength of this yearly greeting. Intermittently he would protest: "I haven't seen any of them for years."

"I daresay, George, but this postmark is London. No distance at all. And she knows that you've moved from the Terrace. Achieved the Crescent. Even her card is growing more expensive."

From the day of his engagement, his relatives had maintained: "Rhoda is the last woman for you. Now if it had been either of the Seton sisters or their nice cousin from Newcastle. Even the Rigby girl would have suited you better." Indignantly he had seized his hat and left the parental roof. Rhoda of these first days, his breezy wind-blown darling, his Diana of dream-uplands—it was outrageous!

Now, as they moved out of the Proclamation crowd, Rhoda helped herself to his arm, and hugging it companionably said: "How baby loves his bit of bunting!" her smile warm, provocative.

Dryly he retorted: "And what does my critic love?"

"George, by the Grace of God," she said promptly. "Let Gwennie look out!"

Was it conceivable that she could maintain this badinage for another year? And if five, why not fifty? From the bottomless pit of her resentment, she might yet elect to refuel for eternity. Imagination boggled at the future which possibility now evoked. If Gwennie should prove a life sentence!

There had only been one way out in 1905. He must anticipate the postman at Christmas. Fortunately Gwennie was invariably early. The feasibility of bribery next presented itself. More cheerfully he faced the year's decline.

Three days before Christmas, Gwennie again flew in

through the letter box, in a larger envelope than usual, and lay there solitary, conspicuous. Halfway down the stairs, he pounced. Instantly he consigned it to the study fire.

At that moment Rhoda's key was heard in the front door. Usually she rang. She must have raced the postman.

Breathlessly she entered. "Anything by the post?"

With hauteur he enquired: "What were you expecting?"

"The man must have left something," she challenged.

"A circular," he said coldly, completely master of the situation.

"Which of course you burned!"

"Naturally . . . er, why not?"

It was the worst Christmas in his experience of her. In fact so dire were her implications, so barbed her innuendos that his New Year resolution was a determination to let nature take its course in future. Suspicion had become conviction, in absence of the body. By its destruction he had simply attested to his own guilt.

The birth of twins in June was the occasion of an uneasy truce. Croup at Christmas partially stole the stage from Gwennie's souvenir, which this year came from Cannes with Continental implications.

Thereafter for three years the twins loyally saved the situation. Alphabetically they proceeded to work their way through every ailment known to man. For three festive seasons Gwennie's devilish persistency glanced off parents haggard with touch-and-go. Then Europe burst into flames. Christmas, 1915, found him in billets near Bethune where the unwelcome tidings reached him from Rhoda: "Gwennie still loves you." A year later in a military hospital en route to Blighty, a belated card from Rhoda merely stated: "Gwennie again." A compression that struck him as sinister. Fortunately on his arrival with influenza from France, he contracted pneumonia. December was removed completely from the map of his mind.

Tottering towards convalescence in February, Rhoda, chastened out of recognition, had almost given him a seizure by tearfully whispering one morning: "Gwennie's downstairs. On the mantelpiece. I've saved her for you, darling."

He was out of the wood. So he thought. Free to enjoy his twins: a stolid pair, by Rhoda flippantly labeled Dods and Dumps. Eleven years old. Time was flying. Soon be Christmas again.

The mildest Christmas they'd ever had; the big house packed with amiable in-laws. Sobered by the war to end wars. Sentimental over his recovery. Peace at last.

Indifference on the score of Gwennie, whose current card now crowned the clock, had reached a point enabling Rhoda to ask his sister Meg at dinner: "Who is—was—she? Can you think?"

"Why, darling, yes of course! It might be any of the three. One was a Seton sister, silent and statuesque. Quite a beauty in her way. A really lovely skin. The other was the Rigby girl, good fun but go-ahead. Ankles you'd remember. The best of the bunch was the Seton's cousin from Newcastle. A prim little girl with a pretty figure. She was known as the Pocket Venus. Men just couldn't resist her."

Rhoda's smile glinted merrily, madly, he couldn't determine which. " 'There was Mary Beaton, and Mary Seton, and Mary Carmichael and me'—so let's have a toast to the survivor, for I mean to see her out!"

On a gale of laughter the family shouted Excelsior! He, who was not averse to a touch of ceremony in his relationships, felt an unmitigated fool, nor was he deceived. The Pocket Venus had sealed his fate. Rhoda, whose figure was Junoesque, could not contain her ire.

Within a month Rhoda had run Gwennie to earth by means of a detective agency. The Pocket Venus, apparently, held a post in the editorial office of a woman's magazine. Coldly he pointed out that Gwennie's laborious signature did not suggest the cursive script of a writer to him.

Astonishingly Rhoda dissolved in tears. It wasn't Gwennie, she sobbed, but something far, far worse. She had overdrawn her bank account. There had been a ghastly misunderstanding over the agency's fees. The detective's expenses had worked out daily instead of weekly as she'd been led to believe.

It was not the first time that an overdraft had brought them together. Then Gwennie struck again. Temporarily united on the strength of Rhoda's solvency, they were discussing Dods' career, when half shyly he said:

"And later I'd like Dods to go to Cambridge."

"Cambridge! Are you crazy? Why your father wouldn't hear of it for you. And Dods hasn't got, will never have your head."

"My head?" to his surprise his voice shook. "This is news from you!"

"News," she scoffed, "that your father was the backbone of the Destructor and that you are the brains?"

The Destructor, he thought savagely, always the Destructor from her! She had just paid him her first and probably her last compliment yet not even on this occasion could she refer to it as the Dreadnought. A name to forge and rivet any engineer's credentials, for only the docks respectfully added the fatal distinction: Sanitary. Not that he was in the least ashamed of the Destructor. He simply did not advertise it, for the skeleton in the

Rennie cupboard, or the golden goose, was a patented portable bin that with a maximum of efficiency and a minimum of residue consumed small rubbish endlessly, and with a safety that satisfied the most captious insurance company. Factories and offices, hospitals and nursing homes were insatiable in their demand for the Dreadnought in all sizes. The din that issued from the Rennie's Yard upon the river suggested the birth of leviathan itself. With the foundry in full blast there was nothing to be squeamish about. If this were not engineering it was tantamount.

In the teeth of present silence, Rhoda recklessly repeated: "Of course you're the brains of the Destructor."

Incensed he shouted: "Dreadnought, damn you!"

Stupefied, she protested: "What's in a name?"

Insanely he roared: "The difference between you and Gwennie!"

Aghast, they stared at one another. Then flinging herself on his breast, she sobbed hysterically: "She's sent us off our heads —I always knew she would!" abruptly breaking off to fetch him a stiff whisky, followed by his dressing gown, and the news that she had telephoned the doctor.

This period was ever after known as Daddy's Nervous Breakdown, but for five years it earned a certain respite. Throughout this time Gwennie, who still foreclosed in December, became a family joke. During this lull in hostilities he found it quite pleasing to reflect on the prim girl with the pretty figure who still remembered him at Christmas. Gwennie naturally never aged, and clearly she was fond of him. Secretly he was half afraid she might fail next year.

It was Dumps, a tactless girl, who ineptly said: "The card's still signed Gwennie, but of course she may have married."

"Rubbish," said Rhoda. "Only a spinster would have the energy for this non-stop performance."

"Miss Marathon it is!" Dods had proclaimed. Thereafter neighbors would politely inquire for her as such.

"Miss Marathon's card has come from Cairo this year," Rhoda informed their friends. "I wonder if she met Tom Fowler!" A reference in poor taste. Fowler had been one of Rhoda's flames. But Rhoda was hipped by the fact that Dods had fallen in love with Betty Hallam, a wealthy stockbreeder's daughter. There was no reason why they should not marry. Dods had always wished to farm. Old Hallam thought a lot of him.

An hour before the ceremony, which took place one year later, Rhoda broke down tearfully—for once the clinging vine.

As they left the house with bouquet and boutonnière, a crowd had gathered in the snow. This was marriage. The postman hesitated on the step. Gwennie's card was served like a summons upon him.

This was romance, for Gwennie had lasted quite as long as his marriage. On a starvation diet too. If ever a woman were self-supporting, it was divinely she! And the flower decked church that morning had set his own dream to music. The choir, hallowed by candlelight, seemed to extol the selfless nuptials of mild but ardent souls. At the opening bars of "O Perfect Love" he could hardly contain his emotion and, glancing aside, was horrified to see his wife, now tearless, winking satirically at him.

Dods had been happily sped.

Very different had been his attitude to Dump's marriage.

"Dumps must marry *now*," Rhoda insisted, "if she's to marry at all. She isn't everyone's cup of tea, but she does seem to be Mungo's."

Mungo, a glum, handsome accountant from Perth had nothing but prospects to offer and an irrelevant Honors in Mathematics. It pained George to see his daughter laying shameless siege to this unsuitable Einstein. And he said so. Day in, day out,

Dumps brooded on the domestic scene. Rhoda's animosity had always sparkled. He found he preferred fireworks to sulks.

"Twin mules," Rhoda explained. "Dumps of course is your double. You may as well give in. I certainly shall. I don't want another undying enemy in this house."

Dourly Dumps carried her day, and plumped for a Registry Office. Gracelessly she announced that Mungo did not possess the fancy dress essential for All Saints.

"Don't be dramatic, Dumps. Your father will lend his morning dress. Leave Mungo to me."

Resentfully Mungo was married at All Saints in George's morning dress. The thing was called a favor.

Again George thought of Gwennie, but only to reflect that many single women lived healthy, happy lives outside his own circle.

As he gave his daughter away to this impecunious young man, he felt he had been burgled in broad daylight—and with the blessing of the Church.

One year later, Rhoda said: "You ought to make a place for Mungo. You can't expect to live forever. Poor dear Dumps!" Now that Dumps was out of the house, she and her mother were thick as thieves. "Mungo is made for the Destructor. Soon he'd be on the Board."

It was exactly what George feared. *Over my dead body,* he resolved.

All over the world, at that instant, millions came to the same decision. And to the minute Europe also declared her hand.

Within six months the Dreadnought's personnel was halved. He could have done with Mungo then, but Mungo and the Black Watch were among the first to go. Despite the farm, Dods left later with the Buffs. Betty could carry on, he said. She had a first-rate head for forms.

It was bewildering. Gwennie's Christmas card somewhat prematurely depicted both dove and olive branch, for within, without, Rhoda gave no quarter. The war had gone completely to her head as she organized the Crescent from his house. Patriotic letters were now penned to the press, which George must punctuate and polish to a deadlier persuasion. She scotched indifference in high places. Sloth and waste were hounded forth. Slander became his specter. The inertia which is any civic center's heart of peace was blown sky high. Hurriedly she was placed on every available committee. Her photograph appeared in the local press. There were editorial requests for articles on "How to Win the War." He was worn out. She was invited to address public meetings at which she delivered George's speeches with a verve and effrontery he could never have achieved. In drafting further orations for what she termed her side of the House, he found himself exposing lethargy in his own party's program. Dismally he was despoiled of the last of his prejudices.

Exhilarated she exclaimed: "I wonder if Gwennie's put on weight. I shudder to think what I'd look like today if I were a pocket edition!"

Ominously he retired behind a smoke screen.

"People," she pursued, "say I should stand for Parliament at the next election."

Paralyzed, he closed his eyes.

The Yard was his salvation. The Foundry his sanctuary. The Dreadnought, like Rhoda, had also come into its own, but on rational lines. In answer to imperative demand, on an island where an exposed light had become a criminal offense, it drew up in unbroken phalanx. Against every possible obstruction, the human element prevailed, and the Dreadnought moved out endlessly on its crusade of cleanliness, a symbol of sanity in a world bent on its own destruction. On advice notes, on Class A certificates, on bills of lading its official name still discreetly figured, but throughout the United Kingdom it had buoyantly become that household word—Rennie's Destructor.

His knighthood was regarded as its crowning achievement. The Christmas speech he shyly made at the Works Dinner was regarded as one of his wife's best.

In the general excitement, Gwennie with her instinct for sympathy thought he'd been made a peer, and addressed her card accordingly.

"The woman's an idiot," said Rhoda. "I always told you so. Out with it, George! *Was* she the one you liked best?"

In view of his damning ignorance a hurricane row was due, but Rhoda spoke almost genially. As if she were humoring him. With a little chill at his heart he suspected her of kindness.

Twelve months passed before she rallied him again: "What's the betting for Christmas? Will Gwennie have braved the bombs in London for another year?"

Gloomily he replied: "Wouldn't like to think of that card stopping now. Hope Gwennie will see me out."

"Not if I can help it!" Rhoda retorted, with a flash of the old spirit, which put them both in better heart, for it had been a heavy year, with the news of Mungo's injuries in Italy. Decorated for gallantry, due home now without a leg. Childish to think that he had once grudged Mungo his morning dress. Childish, and somehow shameful. Already George had cleared the Board Room out. Mungo's office was ready on the ground floor. The others could climb, George among them.

The heaviest year of all, with Dods posted as missing in November.

December with fog further darkening the day! Tomorrow was Christmas, and for the first time in history Gwennie the forerunner for forty years had failed. It was like an omen. Family and friends alike deplored it. Neighbors shook their heads.

Off the afternoon train came Betty in the sloppy slacks that everyone now wore—dry eyed, drawn, restlessly rolling a cigarette. Hovering round the mantelpiece, before she put fate to the touch: "Gwennie turned up yet?"

"There's still time," Rhoda insisted. "What a lot of miseries you are!"

Dully they sat down to tea.

Two false alarms and then the last mail thudded home. Among the lesser fry, the envelope lay there, larger than usual, handsomer than ever. His fingers shook slightly as he withdrew the card and crowned the clock.

Then, and then only Betty's unnatural calm broke down.

"Dear old Gwennie," she sobbed, "always so steady! Whether he comes back, or whether he doesn't, there's always the past to remember!"

Within twelve hours a telegram through the International Red Cross had reached them: *Alive and kicking, Dods.*

Gwennie was canonized!

And in the months that followed, with both boys safe at last, George was forced to face his own misfortunes: six officers and their batmen beneath his hospitable roof. The batmen's radio was getting on his nerves. Gwennie might crown the clock in silent sentiment, but someone called Dinah Shore went round it vocally. Morning, noon, and night, swooners or crooners, whatever they were called, drove him to despair.

"Only a matter of time," said Rhoda, but had the grace to add, "of course the same might be said of any penal sentence." Dinah had shaken her as the worst barrage had not. Dinah had united them as years of marriage had not. For George the crowning virtue in any woman had now become Radio-Inactivity. Horrifying to reflect that he might have married a woman addicted to swing or jive. Even Gwennie . . .

The military moved out. Painters moved in—silent, saintly, white-coated figures who only needed tea and limitless time in order to labor. The end of the war itself was taken in their leisurely stride, came as an anti-climax.

Blissfully George and Rhoda camped out in a denuded drawing room. In this cumulative, this hoarded quiet, he grew to dread his grandchildren. His wife had become for him the only woman in the world.

Benevolently she brought down the old screen from the nursery to keep the draft off. He looked a little bloodless, she said. He could see that she was worried about his health. He welcomed this urbanity. When tolerance is learned between two incompatibles, it can only mean one thing—that daily life like an old slipper has grown too large for one of them. Mungo, he reflected, would miss him more than anyone. Astonishing to think that Mungo now meant more to him than either of his children. Mungo and Gwennie, his two permanent surprises. Yet he could count on them.

"Thirty-nine," said Rhoda, "including this week's card." Briskly she set down scissors, brush, and glue. The children's scraps were peeling off, but she'd soon see to that!

Astounded he stared. She had saved Gwennie's cards. Throughout the years. A thing he'd never thought of.

"Only one short," she reminded him. "The one you burned. Remember? I'll leave a blank to commemorate!"

As Gwennie spread herself upon the screen, the real Gwennie, that composite entity of years, reasserted herself for their affectionate gaze. Ornate and expensive cards, cards denoting bursts of extravagance, periods of prosperity when Gwennie had clearly been cutting a dash. Yet cards also when Gwennie had as clearly felt the pinch. "Or else," Rhoda slapped it on, "this has been one of those years when anything will do for George!" Base supposition! Gwennie's fortunes had varied, he could see that from the cards, but latterly he was glad to note that the cards suggested more than a modest competence! Cards of sentiment, cards of esteem, of reunion, of remembrance. Milestones, too, for now the screen was studded with souvenirs of their worst rows. He flinched at those embossed lilies; the fleur-de-lis emblematic of the wars of their middle ages!

Across thirty odd years Rhoda leaned forward now and tenderly, no, fleetingly stroked his nose with the wet bristles of the glue brush. "I wonder why you hid behind that Trappist vow of silence? I wonder why you didn't tell me which it was?"

"What difference would it have made?"

"I would have been at peace."

"But would she?"

"It was from the one you liked best, wasn't it?"

Defiantly he roared: "Damn you, yes!"

"Meg said that she was prim, but with a pretty figure. It was her figure that attracted you?"

"No!" he shouted, "it was not. It was her gentle nature. I don't admire small women."

Turning a grandiloquent, a lustrous look upon him Rhoda sighed happily, but hungrily: "Now I'm satisfied!" and he had a melancholy conviction that he was doomed to repetition.

Yet there he was wrong.

There wasn't time for reassurance in a nightmare world where emergency operations take place overnight.

Such a shock, the Crescent said, in its letters of condolence.

Since the funeral he seemed to be inhabiting some sort of a vacuum. Rhoda had been a lifelong exasperation. He did not expect to mourn her in the usual way. Nor did he. All was stale, flat, unprofitable—a universe from which the weather had freakishly withdrawn.

In this numb state his children were enabled to enforce their ideas. He must be near them *both,* they said. A flat in London was the very thing. Theaters, museums, galleries, something stirring the whole time. Mungo alone was dubious. Mungo alone had guessed that only one's contemporaries speak the same language and that to make a home, one must first make memories. George missed his cronies in this sprawling tomb of ten millions where something went on all the time.

Unexpectedly his doctor called. Passing through London between trains, he had exactly twelve minutes to devote to George. Fervently he hoped that George would see reason in this time.

"Monte Carlo," he prescribed. "Spring sunshine, change of scene. Mungo says that coastline is the only one on which the Destructor hasn't got a stranglehold. Make a job of the Mediterranean. To mope," he threatened, "would annoy your wife."

Two nights before George left, he listlessly opened an evening paper.

At once attention quickened. The Pocket Venus was front page news! A distinctly pleasing face. Gwennie had weathered well. She didn't look more than thirty. Astonishing!

The well-known novelist, he read, whose latest book *Tomorrow is Here,* recently filmed by Hollywood, now ran into its eightieth thousand, had generously agreed to sign copies of this work for the Displaced Persons' Fund at the Ritz Hotel tomorrow at 4 p.m.

He read the notice again. Hang it all, that was what he was himself now. A displaced person! He ought never to have left the Crescent. Yet if he had remained at home, he would not now be next door to Gwennie, in a place where clearly something went on the whole time.

Tomorrow at four! There would just be time before he left. It seemed like the finger of fate, this opportunity to thank Gwennie without clumsily intruding. The past that had become the present! Merely for a moment, of course. There was no question of the future for a widower of his recent, indeed his immediate standing.

Punctually next day at the Ritz bureau, he inquired for Gwennie, and passed across his card.

"Are you expected, sir?"

"Yes and no," said George. "A call in connection with the Displaced Persons' Fund."

The receptionist bowed and signaled a number on his telephone at the back. Almost at once he replaced the receiver.

"This way, if you please, sir."

Smoothly the elevator opened upon a corridor, opulent, deserted. George had expected a queue chattily winding downstairs or on the mezzanine floor where, inconspicuously, he would have mingled with the cream of eighty thousand readers.

Advancing further into this hinterland of hush and somnolence, he began to doubt the wisdom of these proceedings. But the receptionist was already opening one door and knocking upon another. Gwennie was sealed away, obviously a suite. No expense spared.

"Come in," fluted a distant voice.

The receptionist retreated and George advanced alone into an empty but luxuriously furnished boudoir, sweet with the scent of hyacinths. A fire sparkled in a grate that was also centrally heated. The temperature was tropical. Tea was daintily set for two.

The bedroom door opened and Gwennie issued with out-stretched hands in a negligee, or was it a tea gown? A foam of pink lace that dealt kindly with a figure that had amply fulfilled Rhoda's prophecies. Yet he would have known her anywhere. This lavish greeting recalled his mother's charm at garden-party moments. After forty years in the wilderness, he felt he had come home.

"Good gracious!" between a gasp and a laugh Gwennie had stopped short, as if startled to see him. Well, forty years was forty years! "There's been some mistake."

"Gwennie!" he took her hands, warmed by the pleasant room, her festive appearance, a cordiality that pervaded the whole atmosphere. "Don't you remember me? George Rennie. Reading of the Displaced Persons' Fund, I came along to help."

"But that was yesterday," she protested. "It was all over in an hour."

"Yesterday?" blankly he stared. "I beg your pardon. I must have picked up an old paper."

"Sit down," she said kindly, "for a minute. Your name sounded like Denny on the phone. Tell me where we met."

"At the Boughton ball. Over forty years ago. Don't you remember?"

"Of course I do!" agreeably she dimpled. She did not look more than fifty. Rhoda would have been surprised. "What a dance that was! It's all coming back. You were a friend of Eagle Elliot's."

"Scarcely," he shook his head. "Of course, I know whom you mean. But the real reason of my call is to thank you for the cards—the card signed Gwennie that came each Christmas for forty years."

"A card—each Christmas . . . for forty years? But how amazing—and how sweet. I only wish I'd thought of it. It must have been someone very fond of you."

Hurriedly he said: "There were three Gwennies, which made it more confusing, but Rhoda, my wife, swore you were the one."

"Now I *do* remember," cried Gwennie in triumph. "Of *course!* You're George Rennie who married Rhoda Shelley, the girl with the musical laugh. She and I met at table tennis. Such a merry laugh. I can hear it still."

"My wife," he hesitated to put the dire fact into words, "died three months ago."

"Oh, dear," said Gwennie softly, "oh dear, oh dear! Yes, of course I met you at the Boughton ball. I went there with my cousin Gwen—Gwen Seton!" she exclaimed. "Why, that's the explanation—Gwen must have sent the cards. Not that she ever said a thing. Just a little secretive. She has a villa now at Monte Carlo—Villa *Mille Fleurs.*"

"Monte Carlo!" he expostulated. "But I'm going there tomorrow."

"*Mille Fleurs,*" counseled Gwennie. "Now don't forget. You simply must meet again."

Startlingly, the telephone pealed, but his hostess did not lift the receiver. Nervously, she leaned forward—yes, with a hunted look.

"I hate to hurry you," she blushed, "but I'm afraid I must now say goodby. The *stairs* are on the left."

Gwennie, of all people, and at her age! Distantly he had taken his leave.

The Villa *Mille Fleurs* would be the last place he'd visit! It was, in fact, the first.

As soon as he saw that slender white façade, clustered with pink gereniums, bright with mimosa, he knew that Gwennie was found. In the *salon* where he awaited her, an early syringa graced belated arrival. The air was already sweet with orange blossom.

Gwennie entered in unrelieved black. Six feet tall, of imperial carriage, her classical features were Roman in their reticence.

"Sir George Rennie?" It was not a query. It was a charge for which he must account. She recalled his paternal grandmother —her gravity a reprimand. Rhoda in a rage had been cosy by comparison. Only Rhoda could have dealt with her. It was a judgment.

With some servility he said: "Yes, I hoped you might remember me. We met forty years ago at Lord Boughton's ball. I called today to thank you for the Christmas card which I thought —I hoped you'd sent me ever since."

"You thought, you hoped? Sit down please. I must ask you to explain yourself."

"Forty cards in all. My wife and I valued this kind thought. And as I was in this neighborhood—"

"You say I sent your wife a card for forty years?"

"You sent me a card for forty years. My wife was not at that ball. But of course she too enjoyed the cards."

Coldly Miss Seton enunciated: "Your wife *enjoyed* this eccentricity?"

"Well, you traveled a good deal. The cards were interesting."

Ominously Miss Seton said: "To travel extensively does not mean one *hunts*. I am at a loss to understand your wife. To send a married man greetings for forty years amounts to a pursuit. But it is not one of mine."

Hurriedly he said: "Of course, of course! I have only to meet you to realize my mistake. I trust you will accept my apologies. But through these cards my wife and I grew very fond of Gwennie."

Miss Seton continued to look her unbelief. She might have been deputizing for Rhoda. A scourge of a woman.

"There were three Gwennies at that dance," he insisted. "The only ones I knew. Your cousin, the authoress, among them. I called on her last week. It was she who gave me your address."

"Indeed!" wrathfully she glared at him. "Very typical of Gwendoline. I shall plagiarize Le Gallienne's tribute to Ouida and say: If my cousin had not had hemorrhage of the imagination she would be a genius."

Hastily he rose. "Quite so, quite so!"

"It is apparent," said his hostess coldly, "that if my cousin —I say *if* my cousin did not send these cards, they must have come from Gwen Rigby. Also in our party."

Rather quickly he turned. "So you do remember the ball?"

"Of course I remember the ball," she said shortly. "One is not young forever. I remember you too, Sir George. And there was Elliot Hawke—Eagle Elliot as he was called. With a magnetic eye."

Aloofly George replied: "I'm afraid it's Gwennie who interests me. Do you know what happened to Miss Rigby?"

Stiffly the other answered: "She was not a friend of mine. Merely an acquaintance—" for the first time she hesitated. Without her precision he noticed she looked younger, oddly at sea. "For twenty years I lost sight of Miss Rigby. During the period I was principal of Cheame College. But at the outbreak of the last war, unfortunately, we met again. At the Ladies' Kindred Club, Kensington. Miss Rigby was not a member—latterly. Invidiously she took a room in the block behind at a private hotel called the Pembroke. We kept meeting in the street. It was most embarrassing."

The block behind the Ladies' Kindred Club! Not that he had the slightest intention; an experience like today's would last him a long time.

On a squally September day, a dowdy and reluctant hostelry informed him that Miss Rigby had been gone three years.

Yes, there was another address. But 33 Piggott Place, Brixton, revealed that Gwennie had long since departed for 166 Sentry Street, Louth End, Fulham Way. Obstruction stiffened resolution. By now his blood was up.

In a downpour Louth End was achieved at five o'clock. A district difficult to connect with Fulham or its palace.

For some minutes he walked down a dismal street, between seedy houses, their windows closely screened behind uniformly dirty glass. Some still had the morning's milk upon their doorsteps. Both sides were deserted. There was not even a cat skulking among the garbage bins. At the entrance to Sentry Street, a Salvation Army officer had hurried out, and George remembered a statement of his father's: "They go where no one else will." Yet here was George himself en route. Not often in this country that a street looked so suggestive. Hardly British, yet scarcely French. Too comfortless. This was not a going concern. These houses suggested persons only fitfully in residence. It was difficult to say what could be going on here. Counterfeiters, doing time instead of business, scampered like mice through his mind. Fanciful perhaps. What on earth had happened to Gwennie?

Alarmed he found himself outside her number.

As he rang the bell, in lightning inventory there flashed before him the contents of his pockets: gold watch, gold cigarette case, twenty pounds in notes. A pity!

A middle-aged man in his shirt sleeves, with the biceps of a boxer opened the door. "It's all right, mother," he shouted. "It's for her." Scarcely pausing for Gwennie's name, "Straight up," he ordered. "First room on left." Almost as if George were expected.

Frowning he tapped.

"Come in," said Gwennie.

An old woman with frizzy gray hair sat in a frowsy bed-sitting room, languidly dressing dolls.

"Take a pew," she invited. Only the accent was authentic. It still belonged to the Rigby girl, good fun but go-ahead.

"I see you don't remember me. I must apologize," his embarrassment was patent.

"Not a bit of it," she said. "Probably a long time since your last visit. Which shall it be—cards or the crystal?" Sharply she watched him. "Perhaps a cigarette?" she suggested. "A *friendly* cigarette?"

Something in this reassuring adjective chilled him to the spine. Vigorously he repudiated the idea of a cigarette.

"I simply called to thank you for a kindness, Miss Rigby. We met forty years ago at Lord Boughton's ball. My name is George Rennie."

Stupidly she stared at him. "The Boughton ball? Yes, I remember that quite well. But I don't remember you. What was the kindness?"

"You were one of three girls whom I met that night called Gwennie. The others—Miss Seton and her cousin—both say they did not send the card—the card that came each Christmas since. For forty years. From you, from Gwennie. My wife and I were—were much affected! Forty years is a long time."

"You're telling *me!*" Gwennie grimaced. "But I'm not likely to forget Miss Seton. Thereby hangs a tale! Not one her cousin could write, however! The Boughton ball . . ." she paused. "What a jolly old buffer Lord B. was! Yes, it's all coming back. The flowers, those favors—wildly extravagant, and why not! Such suppers too. Eagle Elliot—the rascal!—used to take me in to supper."

George had risen. "Then you didn't send the cards?"

"My dear boy, you never gave me your address. And then a champagne supper, nothing registers after that! It was probably Gwennie Powys who sent the cards. She came with the Pelhams—not much more than a schoolgirl, but she stands out because she slapped Eagle Elliot. Crack like a revolver shot during the 'Choristers' Waltz.' A little Welsh girl."

A little Welsh girl—he had had enough.

"I don't suppose," Gwennie raised a blurred face on which even rigid lines ran loosely, "I don't suppose you'd care to buy a mascot? Every little helps."

"Of course," his smile was strenuous as he slipped some notes among her work.

For the first time she did not watch him.

"About those cards," she said, "wish I could help. But if you ask me," shrewdly she shook her shaggy head, "it was just a stunt and nothing more. Done to annoy your wife."

He gave a short laugh as he turned to go. "Odd!" he said, "we couldn't explain it ourselves, but that idea certainly never occurred to us."

Back at the flat he was glad someone had lighted a fire. He felt all in. Exasperated rather than intrigued by the thought of an alternative Gwennie still at large. Dejected. Bored.

Poor Gwen Rigby! It was sacrilege to think of her as Gwennie. If the children knew, they would feel outraged on Gwennie's behalf.

He pulled up Gwennie's screen, and sat down. Gratefully he spread his chilled hands to the blaze, his eyes leisurely roving over his collection.

Suddenly he started. Alertly he rose. He had just noticed a remarkable fact. The signature bore the same characteristics throughout. In one case only did it differ: the card at the top of

the screen. Stealthily, but perceptibly, the first card drew apart—
the script of 1905 shrank to a lesser more angular Gwennie.

Infallibly his eye travelled to the empty space which
Rhoda had left for the evidence he had destroyed.

What were her words?

I'll leave a blank to commemorate!

Rhoda had had the last word.

On a roar of laughter, the lost laughter of a lifetime he
shook his fist at it. Heedless of the fact that his wife was now an
angel, "You devil!" he shouted, "You devil!"

There would never now be another card. There could
never now be another card.

The last woman for him, they had said! Yes, the first and
the last. Why they were made for each other as only crossed
swords can be! What affinity could boast this vital encounter, this
winning thrust from the blank she had left to commemorate? His
darling, his devastating Gwennie.

The Mocking Bird

The Mocking Bird

"Ah, sar! Since so many years—one hundred welcomes! Too early? No, no, nevaire too soon! Always, always to the fortunate moment. Yes, sar, here is your table in the corner, awaiting you since last you went. All so quiet, but in twenty, thirty minutes we shall hum like one t'ousand bees for *diner*. No, not since the old *Superbe* at Stresa have we met! Why have I returned since my retirement? Ah, sar, the whim of an idle man who knows but one thing well in life—to wait! For the rest, this is now the toy of my old age, as it was the hard labor of my youth. Zat is the only change. Zat and the swinging sign, sar. You are looking at zat? No other alteration have I made since I return as master but this one thing. The new linen, a detail only, but you will observe the quality, and that too I have caused to be well varnished the painted wooden panels of zat Russian madman Sinesky. Always in the old days when I was but the serving boy, before even I became your waiter, I long ver' much to shelter with good paint these walls. Yes, sar, I have endeavored to conserve the atmosphere antique. No changes radical have I permitted, only the swinging sign.

"You think it dangerous to change the name? I too am superstitious, but for one year now it have been changed and only good fortune have befallen. You preferred it as *The Phoenix?* Ah, sar, I am desolated! Were zis alteration not a dedication, gladly would I alter it for you again. If I will explain? But certainly, while Monsieur waits. It is a strange story, but it may pass time for you . . .

"I change this place, sar, from *The Phoenix* to *The Mocking Bird* in memory of two patrons who have absorbed much thought of mine. I change the name in memory of them, for they prove to me who could never have guessed without them that the phoenix is a mocking bird.

"We know so well we change, sar, as the phoenix, daily, yearly, for only then can we pass on as is so necessary, that sometimes the truth escapes us that there are others living in this world who are not as we. Immortals still on earth. So rare are they, zat whole lives may pass and nevaire know them. My history is surely remarkable for in it I have the privilege to meet two of these curious persons who do not change as we. And because of them it is that I have changed my sign, for they have become my legend.

"Yes, sar, in the days when first you came, they came also. But, no, nevaire did you see them for always they dined later. *Mon dieu!* I have seen them come within as late as midnight for their meal. But always they have it, sar, for my dear master, Herr Weber love them much (*Hélas,* yes, sar. The first year of the war, by inches in this very place. Impossible it was to reconcile himself that we should so betray ourselves in pain and death when the great wish of all his life was but to feed and make others *confortable.* And when they cease to eat here and the rooms they empty, only Jacob remaining, then he dies. No, nevaire, nevaire more perfect maître d'hôtel, and yet, amazement is—of Austria. And how he love the English—like a good father! How often before the bad days have I not heard him say, 'Assuredly God is wiz them, how udderwise could they survive their methods!') Yes, sar, often have I watched him pour himself at twelve o'clock the Liebfraumilch of Monsieur and Madame, for fear the police might pass that window there. That was their table, sar, one side by wall and window. Always she must sit there whether dangerous or not with hock at midnight. Always from the beginning she was just a *leetle* exigent, sar. But then, too, the stove chimney from below it runs behind the wall there, and I think perhaps the seat there gave her the warmth she always needed. And Monsieur, sar, all he cared for was zat she should be happy, for from the first evening they come here—a winter night with a great flurry of snow—it was clear as glass to everyone that they love much.

"Ah, sar, I have seen many faces. In this life of mine one has the opportunity, but these two persons were unique. One would have singled Monsieur out from one hundred handsome men. And Madame? I have seen several women more beautiful, sar, even in this room, but when she was here, there was no other woman. And yet it was not this alone that made them both remarkable, but a strangeness and a beauty in the air when they meet together. Their names? Ah no, sar, you will pardon me. I do not speak of them as news. You, sar, are my oldest patron. I reveal them only to my oldest patron and simply as my legend.

"You think I am romantic? Well, you shall judge, but that glamor in the air around them, it was there for all to feel, and all remark. Aura of happiness you say? No, sar, zat it was not. They were the unhappiest people I have ever seen, even when bright and gay. Yet always there was this witchery round them. Everyone who see them, even for space of one meal, look and nod and make a story.

"Perhaps I dream a little because so long ago? But it is true, sar. When Monsier-'Dame came bright and gay here—the room and all within it, sparkle, the flowers smile, the dishes gleam and all feel comfort and content. Yes, festive, sar, we all feel festive when Madame smiles. But of a charm! Not one hundred blooms but the garden itself, for she possess more than sweetness. That, *hélas,* sar, was the reason for what should happen afterwards, that she have more than sweetness.

"And just as surely, sar, when Monsieur-'Dame came cloudy to us, then everything go wrong. The patrons they are *difficile,* the waiters clumbsy—the magic of Monsieur-'Dame reach even to the cook who insult us all, and pour his sauces down the sink with spite. Bad for business, then? Yes and no, sar. For always through it, people wonder of them this and zat and I have known many come again, flattered to sit next them, picturing them as this or zat celebrity. But they were wrong. Nevaire, nevaire were two more private. Even I, their most constant *garçon,* catch little of their talk in all their many times. But there was one phrase I grow to know and to deplore, for always it bode thunder in the air. Madame would draw back her head, and say with ice in every word—'Really!—I must ask you—.' Zat was all, 'Really!—I must ask you—.' But it was enough. Then Monsieur would lean forward, and say with a pleading gentleness, most amiable in a face chiseled so severely—'If only you would be reasonable—.' Zat was all, 'If only you would be reasonable—.' But it was enough, for, sar, I could have told you from my first glance at Madame, in spite of all the ignorance of my situation, that Madame would be everything in heaven and upon this earth but that one thing— reasonable—and of a consequence that Monsieur was as unreasonable to expect otherwise.

"But Monsieur, it is difficult to explain, sar, with all his sympathy, he yet has no imagination beyond one given point. One could tell that alone from the way he order food—a meal chosen with taste, sar, but always the same. Month in, month out. Incredible? But so.

"For months I watch him demanding of her with a persistence exhaustive this one thing she could not give. I believe, sar, it was this fixity of Monsieur's that arose their crisis—for it imposed on Madame a need of equal fixity and she was not made for that. No, she was, for all the stateliness of head and shoulders, as restless as a flame, as full of drama as a playhouse. And drama—one follows—Monsieur could never understand but from a *fauteuil,* and in its proper place. Sometimes I see that Madame knows this, but nevaire does she seek to modify the situation. Oh, no, sar, nevaire! That was the predicament of Madame, for though I think she have more magic than Monsieur to see all round and through a thing, yet never have she got enough to bring her own release. Always is she under her own spell.

"Long before the crisis arrive, I see it in advance upon them—and I tremble, for by this time I have them both at heart. Lastly their meals are but a travesty, for no matter if they started with pale sunshine, they ended of a certainty with storm, so zat the wonder was they came at all together.

"And I must admit it. Madame was the aggressor. Yes, upon each occasion. So that often I felt angered and resentful for Monsieur while they were here. Yes, between soup and savory I would feel all reproachfulness against her. Yet, after they were gone—that was the thing perplexing—this feeling against her, it dissolved. And I would find myself considering, considering. . . . For to me it was a riddle, zis hidden reason why Madame should look at Monsieur as she sometimes did, and why Monsieur should bear so much. Yet I could not rid myself of the conviction even then, sar, young as I was, that although Monsieur was superior, yet that hers would be the finer flights. Both had the air, you understand—the air authentic, but with a difference. This very difference it was that marked them off from others, and, *hélas,* themselves. How can I explain? Well . . . he have poise and she have dignity. Ah, sar, there you have it! His air worn negligently, ze thing of custom and of habit to those born—what is your phrase —in purple? Yes. But hers was ze stiffer dignity that comes of difficult things sustained at a cost, ze cost that impoverishes while it refines.

"It came at last, sar. The final meal—after which they come no more.

"For two, three months I look for them each evening, but in vain. Herr Weber can but shrug his shoulders, until, as is the way of things, the clientèle cease even to remark their absence.

"Time passes and I have ze opportunity of new opening for myself. It is deeficult to go, but yet such things must be. And so I attend zat autumn at Murray's in Piccadilly. For the first year I assist in the Grill Room there. Ah, sar, a place most different from *The Phoenix.* The best of everything in the worst of taste! But I suffer it, for always it is necessary to improve oneself.

"Six months am I there when I receive a great astonishment, for as I enter late the dining room one evening, I am faced to face with Monsieur about to leave! Delighted I hasten forward to his assistance—Monsieur! But, ah, sar! Never shall I forget the expression in his eyes as he remembers me. Even to address me it takes him several seconds longer than was natural. Nevaire have I seen a face so blank, a manner so mechanical. 'Henri,' he said, 'this is unexpected! How are you?' And for a few minutes he talk in a kindly way, but all ze time as if he were himself abstracted from the situation. As I listened to him my anxiety it mounts. A small dread that have come upon me when I see him close, it suddenly increases. I feared to ask how Madame was and yet I was impelled. 'Madame!' he said, drawing his shoulders high like soldier on parade, 'Madame is dead.' And he turned himself and went upon that word. But, sar, even before he have pronounced it, I had known it.

"To another it will be fantastic the effects his news have on me. Even I myself did know it was too momentous for my occasion, and a stranger. Yet these things happen when one is young. For long afterwards my mind was melancholy as if one had removed the only thing of beauty in it.

"But, sar, you know how it is? Time passes and the generous energies of such emotions, they pass too. The next ten years were busiest in my life. And with the passing of the years, faces grow dim in the eye of the mind.

"So, gradually, did the faces of Monsieur and Madame dim for me—with the hundreds of new faces each day imposes on me, by week, by month as I move from one hotel in Europe to the next—for, much as I deplore ze uprootings, ze partings, ze broken friendships that have to come with all such changes, yet invariably have I permitted these. Yes, yes, though it has meant for me many things left by the way.

"And yet, although I do confess they grow dim for me, nevaire did I forget Monsieur—Madame. From time to time, the thought of them return to me, and then for two, three days together I would picture to myself the chance of seeing Monsieur again, for sar, that is the curious thing about the life of any maître d'hôtel. No matter how long the procession of new peoples, there comes a day when one realizes of a certainty that they have *begun to repeat themselves.* Ah, yes, sometimes in ze strangest places. But this, sar, does not happen till middle age. Until then, one is astonished to see ze known face at the other side of the world, but with the years there comes this feeling of inevitability. The covers are laid, as it were, and one awaits.

"Long afterwards I understand clearly zat I have in secret

awaited Monsieur in each hotel and every restaurant I have attended.

"Then one night, ze strangest event of my experience takes place. It was the climax of the season, the second that I am maître d'hôtel at the Hotel Majestic on the Lakes—one year exactly before I have the final good fortune which enabled me to buy ze old *Superbe* at Stresa. It is nine o'clock at night and crowded—*diner* well advanced. Suddenly through the big glass doors there enters Signor Varomini, the proprietor, with a party of eight. At once I note they must be clients of importance. The next moment I am rooted to the spot with my astonishments. There, sailing across the floor in a glimmer of satin and pearls was Madame! Sar, I give you my assurance it was the amazement of my life!

"For the hour she remained seated at that table, I can hardly take my eyes from her, yet I leave it to Verlo to approach her table in my stead. I cannot describe my excitement, the confusion of my feelings, or the sensations of enrichment I receive that I should still be capable of these. No, no, sar, you misunderstand me! Do not suspect me of romantic vaporings, this is no story of love sickness, and a poor mortal. It is, as I have already told you, ze legend of two people who proved to be immortal. And ze truth of what later came to pass, you, sar, will afterwards accept as more than just my fable. I have no place in it. Only am I able to relate it, more closely, it is possible, than most who watched them, for though I have experience only of the lot of most men and have known love and passion—and ze separate state of marriage—yet in my own case zis trinity of passion, love, and marriage, it come together, and zis always makes for complications ver' instructive. So zat is why perhaps I understand Madame at last as I watch her entertain her guests zat night.

"As I look upon her there, I see the years have left less

mark upon her than could have been believed, for with presumption sar, I do confess Madame was ever in outward mold reverse of what I hold to be most admirable in woman's beauty. Always have I admired the dark woman with the shadowy eye and clear cut feature—ze classic type. And Madame was fair, with mobile features which, as they registered each finest shade, ze years might well have punished. But though distinctly I could see a shadow stained below her eyes, yet her face had only gained zat hint of subtle modeling that comes when the mind it have sustained its endless agitations, and have modified the flesh. Ah, sar, the touch austere of time when first it falls upon a vivid face—it may enhance and also fascinate. None is there in that great room but is aware of her proximity.

"When finally she rose to go, all eyes they travel with her to the door, where I stood at attention. I could not, dare not hope she would remember me, for, sar, no longer was I ze stripling waiter of *The Phoenix*. Of a necessity I had had to travel fast, and many changes had been wrought in me.

"As I bowed her out, she looked at me. She stopped short. Her eyes go over me like lightning, and she let her guests stream past. 'Why, Henri!' she exclaimed, 'How *splendid!*' That was what she said, sar. 'Why, Henri! How *splendid!*' but it was not her words that warmed me through like wine. It was her look. In the instant her eyes travel my face, I see she realize it all—ze struggle, ze uprootings, ze good friends left by the way, all ze difficult things that have brought me my success—for always she was zat one person out of every hundred who is—how you put it—aware. Sar, I was at zat time of life then when I begin to wonder how much worthwhile it all have been. But that night I am triumphant, for Madame's look was like a decoration awarded.

"Seven, eight minutes she stand to speak with me, and I am on the heights for while she talks with me of what the years have brought me, it appears as if all were of new significance. For that was ever the effect of Madame, sar—at her touch all became momentous, for the moment, as when music sounds. And she have gone before I realize all this is but her magic.

"That was the last time I saw her there. But, no, sar, I did not ask that question. I had known from the first minute my gaze alight upon her there—from ze bright and measured look behind her eyes, that she had refuge now only in the compensations of existence. I knew as I had watched her entertain her party—as clearly as if I myself had seen her close his eyes—that Monsieur was dead. *Non, hélas,* it was not necessary to ask what all her calm proclaim.

"After that night I cease to look for her again. Something told me then that they had gone for good. . . .

"And now, sar, I come to the curious climax of my story. Eighteen months after this last meeting with Madame, I become, as you know, proprietor of the old *Superbe* at Stresa. Sar, you know yourself the old *Superbe.* You saw it at its heights. Five years with me it is admitted the *première* hotel in Europe. This brings me satisfaction? Well . . . but of course. Yet sometimes I myself am haunted like all who hasten overmuch and the idea persists that it have come too late. But nevaire are we satisfied, and possibly all came too soon, for now I have my leisure—behold! I cannot use it.

"No, sar, ze only satisfaction my wealth has brought me is when I buy this place again where once I served, poor and unknown. I find it sunk to a shabbiness indescribable. Almost I become young again in my haste to renew its charm. Sar, I have spent t'ousands on it. Night after night it fills, but nevaire will it pay now. It is not a business venture. No, no, sar, it is a whim, a dream, run always at a loss.

By fifth of December last year all was finally completed,

ze decorations finished, ze lanterns lit, ze covers laid. At an early hour I come, before even the cook—I come, for I am anxious over this new child of mine! Yes, sar, so anxious almost it is as if the years between, they have not passed. As if this truly were my first venture and not my last. You may not have remembrance, sar, but the fifth of December last year it is a night of most excessive cold. I order Adolf to put up the big screen, but yet to leave the front door open. 'We have warmth and to spare,' I say. 'Let the street have some to bring us luck.'

"For one hour I make a hundred small adjustments, and rub my hands for all seems excellent, most excellent. Then, sar, as early as seven-fifteen I am surprised to hear a car draw up, and I hurry myself to welcome. The next minute through my open door, in a flurry of snow, I am struck dumb to see two faces wreathed in the felicity that have made memorable my first day here! My knees they tremble and I think I dream. For the first time in my life, sar, I forget my duty. I stand rooted to ze spot as they do. In that look we then give it seems as if we know all things of each other. Monsieur and I—we gaze and gaze—till Madame break the spell. She hold out her hand to me, 'Henri, my friend,' she said, 'twenty minutes after seven—angels passing over us.' Her voice recall me to myself, I hurry them into the warmth to the best table which was always theirs. I take their wraps, I get a foot-rest, I send for choicer flowers. *Mon dieu!* I compose within my soul a dinner for them fit for gods. Their gay voices are like music to me as they make note of each new detail. I draw ze curtains. I shut ze windows. I bring a fan. . . . Then after the necessary compliments exchanged, I hasten to the kitchen. And there I tell my chef, 'Above are two patrons who were here in Herr Weber's day. They tell me they ate then a dinner never since surpassed. What do you think?' And so, I do inflame him, then hasten to the cellar.

"Ah, sar, Monsieur had ordered a dinner, but it was not the one he ordered that he got! Monsieur and Madame had a dinner that night I have never equaled—and since that night the trouble my cook have been! At nine o'clock *The Phoenix* it is full, but that one night, for all the time I give myself entire to Madame and Monsieur. And all is as of old, for once again they lend their air of curious beauty to ze place, and all enjoyment it is heightened. The other guests they steal of their festivity, for once again they look at Monsieur-'Dame and nod, and make a story. All is as before.

"Each course in its perfection I set with my own hands before them. But, no, sar, never do they realize what they are eating, for the English eat only with the jaws and in abstractions—no, nevaire do they use the brain for food. Monsieur and Madame they appreciate as ever the attention and the trouble, but the food itself—no, sar, they did not understand it what it was. Yet it was necessary that they had the best, you understand.

"Myself I cannot tell you of my happiness that night! For you will appreciate it, sar, that I was of that time of life when one ceases to expect the unexpected, when ze miracle—always it is too easily explained! And it was one such charming thing that they should come that night of every night. The thing was like a fairy tale—and just because I was both old and tired, the precariousness of ze occurrence, it enchanted me. I could have sung, I could have danced and kissed all people on both cheeks.

"Then, sar—but I can hardly tell you! At nine o'clock it was, ze terrible thing occur at close of *diner*. Just as I enter from the buffet in time to pour the old brandy of Monsieur's liqueur, the calamity take place. As I advance behind their table, I am astounded to behold Monsieur and Madame staring at each other as if petrified. His brow is set, and her chin is high and I am just in time to hear those fatal words again—words set in ice to kill—

I must really ask you— . . . Sar, zis I say—that all states are
natural and to be borne—with one exception—zat frigid poison
which none can counteract—neither he who suffers it, nor he who
does administer it. And for Monsieur and for me it was gathered
for all time in to zese five words of scorn. Sar, I tell you wiz
solemnity, that in my exasperations and despair had I been Monsieur then I would have stabbed her to the heart.

"As soon as I hear the words, as soon as I hear them fall,
freezing ze warmth and comfort—I turn my head away and leave
the room at once. For me, I know it is impossible to look upon
them further. My pleasure, all my happiness, it is gone, pouf, like
smoke! Adolf must look after them.

"As I mount the stairs, my head it aches and I know the
reaction of my foolish earlier excitements. I open the top window
in the passage and lean over the cold street. The lights wink in
the darkness, the snow swirls, the motors flash by endlessly. All is
perpetual motion, eternal change, and for the first time I admit to
myself then that life is too much fuss for nothing.

"Then, sar, just as I think this there is a stir below. I hear
the porter's whistle. A car draws up, and mechanically I watch
Monsieur and Madame enter. But my lively interest in them of so
many years, it has gone with the ebb and flow of other things,
leaving me drained of all but ennui. They are hidden from me in
the darkness of the car. I can see only their knees. And I say to
myself as I look, *'Non,* dead from that point upwards. These people never existed.'

"Then the car jerks, but as it starts, I start forwards too,
till I am almost out from the window! There in the darkness of
the car I see Monsieur's hand go out, and suddenly draw Madame's
hand onto his knee, then not a fraction's pause and she has given
her other as well—while the car streams round the corner, with
them bound once more together—leaving me laughing, sar, as I

have never laughed before! No, not in all my life! I laugh till
I am helpless, till the sides ache, and the tears pour from the eyes,
till Jacob mounts to know if I am ill. But I cannot answer, I can
only laugh and stare down at the sign of *The Phoenix* rising always renewed from its ashes, for at last I see I have found two
people who will never change as we. At last I know their secret.
Always will they love, always will they quarrel, always will they
forgive, eternally secure in zis charmed cycle of the two lovers
immortal. For how is it possible that even death shall divide them
when ze worst of life and themselves have failed?

"That, sar, is why the day following I change my swinging sign from *The Phoenix* to *The Mocking Bird*. It is my tribute
to their legend.

"You smile, sar! The drop of water that wears away the
stone? Ah, that is another story! You think that even yet they will
wear each other out? That they will cease to forgive? And will
change and pass on like others? Well, I am too old perhaps to be
certain of anything, but I have my imaginations on some things.
Ah, yes, sar, you think? Well, perhaps, it may yet be as you say.
Almost it is a year now, well, thirteen months to be exact, but
still I have the feeling—*Sapristi!* Jacob!—Adolf! Attention!
Mille pardons, sar! You will excuse!—

"Eh, *mon dieu! Mon dieu!* Since a hundred years! No, no!
Nevaire too late!—One *t'ousand* welcomes, Monsieur—Madame!"

Lady Penny Goes Too Far

Lady Penny Goes Too Far

The Duchess gave a sigh of relief—she had at last achieved an evening for herself! She was nothing more than a glorified almoner, an over-worked organizer, an unpaid treasurer —appealing for this, inspecting that, assessing here, reporting there!

A satisfaction, however, to have secured that post in New York for the vicar's daughter. If only the poor girl had been going out to an American! Secretary-companion to anyone as insular as elderly Hester Pratt would be no joke. But it might lead to something better. Perhaps a husband?

The October night was as warm as summer, and the tall windows stood wide open upon Regents Park, dark now against the old-rose brocade, the velvet of the vast drawing room, its treasures a-gleam in the soft light of alabaster lamps.

More cheerfully she sipped her after-dinner coffee. Then her face shadowed again. She was remembering a much less satisfactory orphan than the vicar's dutiful daughter. Her own late husband's second cousin, half a dozen times removed, yet ever too near for comfort—Lady Penny Tollmache.

Impatiently the Duchess looked up.

Briggs stood in the doorway, and she had not rung. She had not even finished her coffee.

"Your Grace, I'm sorry to disturb you, but Lady Penelope Tollmache is here. I explained that your Grace was resting, but her ladyship states that the matter is urgent. And indeed, your Grace, her appearance is a little strange."

"Strange?" the Duchess frowned.

"Yes, Your Grace. Her ladyship is covered with dust."

"Show her in," the Duchess said briefly.

And there she was—a flaxen-haired girl, hatless, dressed in russet jeans, Robin Hood shirt, and a tan jacket. The clothes were modishly cut, but carelessly worn, and her shoes were white with dust. In fact, as the Duchess noted distastefully, Lady Penny's unspeakable jeans were also powdered to the knees.

Then the newcomer smiled, and the handsome Duchess suffered momentary eclipse, for this was beauty herself with a dazzling skin, enigmatic eyes, and a sulky seductive mouth. Beauty twice-armed, for the blonde girl was, first and foremost, youth, offhand and self-sufficient.

"Sorry to barge in," she had seated herself with her deplorable legs out-stretched, as if in final exhaustion, "but I thought you'd want to know at once."

"Know what?" the Duchess said coldly.

"That I'm willing to go to New York this week after all. Did you cancel?"

"No, I hoped you'd come to your senses before I again upset Mrs. Bell's arrangements."

"That's that, then."

"I fail to see why you couldn't have telephoned, instead of arriving in this get-up."

"You've got something there," Lady Penny agreed. "But I had to see you once more before leaving."

"Your absence," the Duchess retorted, "would have been understood, after your recent exploits."

The girl straightened herself in the chair. "Ha!" she exclaimed satirically, "let's get the police news straight first. I admit that I ought not to have been in that dive at all. But I'd always wanted to see a gambling hell, and I thought that Ralph and Sally Townley were pretty reliable. After all, they're newly married. The three of us had positively no idea that the others were going to start strip poker. And it was quite the most revolting anti-climax when the police walked in, as we walked out."

"This scandal," the Duchess' voice was icy, "follows rather too closely on your affair with Mr. Beckles."

"Yet nothing happened there either."

"As far as appearances go, everything did. So, if what you say is true, you have simply lost your reputation for nothing."

"I daresay," Lady Penny said moodily. "But that's all that's gone. And, of course, I'm glad in a way——"

Aloofly the Duchess ignored this. "Your behavior has been inexcusable. Your cousin Ardlyon must be disgusted."

"You needn't lose sleep over that. I wouldn't marry Ardlyon now if he were the last man left on earth."

"I wasn't aware that he had asked you to."

Lady Penny laughed. "One up for you—he hasn't."

"Have you dined?"

"I'm not hungry. I had sandwiches earlier in a pub at Richmond. I've been walking since eight this morning."

"You've walked for *twelve* hours!"

"I've been thrashing things out, and I scarcely noticed. Georgiana, I've had an extraordinary experience. Last night— Sunday. I can't hope you'll understand, but it's got to be said. It's feeble to be ashamed to admit it! Whether you believe it, or not, I was converted last night."

The Duchess started, and on a note of derision inquired: "You were *what?*"

Penny nodded. "I'd been feeling like suicide for a week, and Minx Travers, who's been through everything since Bill was missing in Korea said: 'You simply must come and hear Mr. Hale—it's quite a small church in Shepherds Bush, but it is packed every Sunday night.' Well, I couldn't have cared less, for I'm not an emotional type like Minx, but I went. And I was amazed. The man answered every question I'd been asking for years. For instance: Why should I have the advantages I have? Why should *you*, for that matter?"

Frigidly the Duchess said, "That is not the point."

"Well, it's mine."

"And a wholly self-centered one, as usual. The only issue of importance is: What are you doing with these self-evident privileges?"

"Precisely nothing."

"Again you're mistaken. You are doing a great deal of harm. Even now you are wasting time and energy, mine as well as your own."

Penny laughed softly. "Now that you've got that off your chest, let's get back to my conversion."

"My dear Penny, conversion is the answer to an irresistible desire to be other than we are—for a new life, above all a new personality. It is often the natural outcome of final wretchedness."

The girl looked at her steadily. "That's a pretty accurate description—but an address is always less than the place itself! The first thing Mr. Hale said was that mortal existence was death, which I'd often suspected, but didn't want to believe. What he said *next* explained everything."

"How very reassuring."

"Yes, it simplified everything to discover that it's I who am all wrong. It makes it manageable. As it's I who am wrong, I can put everything right—for myself, I mean."

Uncharitably the Duchess exclaimed: "Egotism again!"

"Yes and no," Lady Penny amended, "for now we're coming to the snag in the new situation. After insight, there comes discipline, and finally what he calls a conformed will. With these three tests behind one, he promised that reality will appear. And as he spoke, I *knew* he knew."

"Young people," the Duchess glanced away, "do have these experiences sometimes."

"But I'm not young," her visitor protested. "I'm a ghastly twenty-two. Recently I found I'd lost my political convictions as well. All my instincts are left wing, but at times even my own party seemed to stink faintly. For quite a bit I've wanted an explanation, and on Sunday I got it! Yes," Penny added almost with surprise, "now I'm at peace. Between times, I've a feeling of joy that laps in like little waves. Have you never noticed that even on the shore of a lake the waves seem to be saying: *coming, coming, coming?*

The Duchess remained silent.

"Of course," brooded Penny, "I saw in a flash that conforming the will would be my trouble. So I decided to tackle this right off. And make a sacrifice. That's why I'm here tonight to say I'll go to New York."

Acidly the Duchess said: "This must certainly be the first time in history that Cornelia Bell's hospitality has been regarded as martyrdom."

Impatiently the other recrossed her outstretched ankles. "You miss the point again. I don't *want* to spend three months with a millionairess. I know I haven't met her, but I suspect the worst. One's own set always criticize one, and resent one. It's a relief to walk out and pick up people who may prove easily disposed, who have no ulterior motive."

The Duchess stared. Where was the confidence of youth—youth who might know all this, but, as a rule, healthily didn't care?

"Money as such," Penny continued, "doesn't mean a thing to me, even though I've got none of my own. Of course, I've got certain social advantages. You, for instance. I used to say: Why should I be so lucky? *I know what I am.* That's what made me suspect the whole set-up. But now—since last night—I know. I see I haven't been lucky. Those in the midst of the other things are at another stage altogether."

"I notice you don't offer to join them! In hospitals, or camps for displaced persons, where help is urgently needed."

Again the girl looked at her steadily. "No, I mean to have a shot at something that's within my range first. That's why I'll accept the invitation you've fixed for New York."

This reply, unanswerable as sanity, silenced the Duchess.

"Now that I look at you again," Penny pursued, "I see what's wrong with *you!*"

"Are you referring to *my* need of salvation?"

"Yes, you ought to do something about your hair. Have it cut off, then get a feather cut. You could still be quite terrific if only you'd stop dressing like the last days of Queen Alexandria."

"Thank you!" the Duchess' cheek had flushed.

Penny rose, rather stiffly, from her chair. "When do I leave—for New York, I mean?"

"On Wednesday or Thursday. You'll know tomorrow when you pick up the tickets here."

"Wednesday?" the girl stared. She looked paler now that she was standing. "Oh, well . . . always ready to leave for Mars at a moment's notice."

"Perhaps," the Duchess said irritably, "that's why you haven't arrived yet. You *are* Mars."

Again the girl considered her. "All right, Venus," she said, "don't get uppity! I'm as good as gone."

Perfunctorily they kissed.

"Once this scandal has blown over," the Duchess added, "I hope you'll return to happier times here. That mews apartment was a great mistake—I blame myself there. It's a pity that you've never been able to hold down any work."

"I could have held down any job as driver-secretary—and you know it, only you wouldn't let me accept my continental offers."

"I should think not! But with your fever for travel I can't understand why a first visit to New York should bore you in advance."

"Poor old Europe's good enough for me."

"Perhaps America may yet surprise you."

Penny grimaced, "I don't doubt it!"

It was noon when Penny next rang the Duchess' front-door bell.

She was still hatless, but as she now wore a suit sponsored by Bradley, at the Duchess' expense, she presented a very different appearance.

"Good morning, Briggs, anything for me?"

As he handed her, on the old, engraved salver, an envelope bearing her name, she inquired for the Duchess.

"Her Grace is not at home, your ladyship."

"Any idea where she is?"

"I believe Her Grace has gone to the hairdresser's."

"Bejabbers she has!" Lady Penny was amused. "Then is that model of efficiency Miss Frant available?"

"No, your ladyship. Her Grace's secretary has gone to the dentist, after much pain. Miss Frant has not been herself for some days."

"Too bad!" condoled the visitor. "Comforting, though, to know that the infallible are also human. They have hair, likewise teeth. This is goodby then, Briggs. Positively my last appearance. I'll send you a postcard from the top of the Empire State Building."

She sauntered down the steps.

Briggs, with a bow, closed the door. He considered Lady Penny a great pity. That was as far as he would let himself go in disloyalty.

Dawdling along Cumberland Terrace in autumn sunshine, Lady Penny ripped open the large envelope, and with a lackluster eye discovered that she left London airport Flight 57 tomorrow evening. The ticket was on Tourist Airways.

"Tourist!" she muttered. "On my first flight too! Georgiana's certainly getting a bit frugal in her old age. Oh, well, who cares!"

Unfolding a sheet of the Duchess' elegant writing paper, she noted her future address on Park Avenue, New York.

But who the dickens was Miss Pratt?

Her frown faded. She remembered now. The Duchess had told her to telephone Mrs. Bell's secretary on arrival at the airport.

"Try to give as little trouble as possible." Miss Pratt must be the secretary.

Well, that was that.

And now that, for once, she was doing the right thing, she could forget all that these unwelcome details meant—and get back to her growing peace, to that incredible but deepening joy, in which the little waves of some invisible tide said, *coming . . . coming . . . coming.*

Lady Penny awoke on the Tourist airliner as breakfast was being served. She had passed a more comfortable night in her adjustable seat than she expected, and after a hearty meal could not explain a growing depression.

Overnight she seemed to have lost her new-found peace. The serenity that had altered the world for her, since her conversion, had treacherously vanished after launching her on this journey of sacrifice! En route to New York, in faithfully following its behest, it had left her high and dry. Literally! Only for the moment, of course, but none the less, bad enough!

Glumly, she noticed yesterday's neglected evening paper sticking out of her satchel, and lest her unknown companion should get into conversation, she hastily drew it out.

At once she caught sight of a headline:

Lord Ardlyon's Pedigree Perseus wins Cattle Show Award.

Bully for him, she punned ironically, but her heart had already betrayed her by a painful lunge.

Six-foot-three, he had suddenly obliterated the miles between them, and the airliner itself. His hair, burnished bronze, revealed the commanding brow and clean-cut features of family tradition. But his caressing smile was his own, and those piercing eyes—which in color alone resembled Penny's much lovelier ones.

(101

"My two Norse invaders," so Cousin Ida, his mother, had fondly dubbed the young people on childhood holidays in Scotland.

Seven years Penny's senior, Ardlyon had been her hero since she was twelve and known him resplendent in his Scots Guards uniform. This phase had lasted till she was sixteen. At that stage it hadn't mattered a jot that he guessed—so tender had been his teasing, so merry his raillery. He had singled her out. Anybody could see. At seventeen, she still burned a candle to him in her heart, although they so rarely met. But at the Glenor-land wedding, although she wasn't officially "out," and only a poor relation, and her best frock perfectly frightful, again his glance had extolled, and his words had rallied her. At that theater-dinner afterwards, there had been at least three full-blown debs permanently soured by this! "Who's the overgrown schoolgirl in auntie's back number?"

How Penny blazed to show them!

And she had—two years later, when the Duchess took her clothes in hand, and launched her upon London. But by then it was too late. Ardlyon was in Australia, visiting his sheep farm. He missed the sensation she had caused. What he heard at second-hand apparently left him cold! On his return he didn't exactly ignore her, but his tribute was a trifle jocular. As one might humor a relative or a nitwit! Under these circumstances it was, of course, imperative to answer his raised eyebrow with a challenging smile, or a sophisticated shrug. Latterly, to avoid him pointedly—for not once did he attempt to take her around himself. He simply watched her from a distance. Finally, scarcely that . . . his aloofness was a kind of affront. She was still so much his at heart, that his critical detachment first alarmed and then antagonized her. Especially as Ardlyon had a flair for turning up at some restaurant, or gala per-formance, where her own escort was unsuitable, or her party row-dily inclined. She grew to detest his smiling superiority, and deliberately went gay—in the dismal way that young things did in post-war London, where Bohemia had become methodical, and even the drinks were ersatz. Soon the press took a hand, as if equally anxious to finish Ardlyon off. Her photograph popped in and out of the evening papers with each fresh craze.

One break only she had had! A fortnight before that police court adventure, things began to come right. Cousin Ida arrived from Scotland, and Penny was invited to dine at Claridge's. Cousin Ida, who might easily have passed for an angel had it not been for a devastating sense of humor, always brought Penny luck!

That evening, exhilarated, Penny had skipped out of her bath. It was highly possible that within a few hours, she and Ardlyon would dance at last! Strangely enough, they had never done so yet. And on the dance floor Penny knew herself to be a passport to paradise. She had been told so often enough!

In a blissful whirl she dressed, but entered Claridge's as pale and poised as a pearl . . . in shell-pink marocain with one mink shoulder-knot. Just right!

"Breathlessly beautiful!" he greeted her on the threshold. His voice had its new note of mockery, but his eyes, their old tenderness.

"My dear child," Cousin Ida assured her over iced cantaloupe, "in an earlier era people would have stood on tables to see you! What a pedestrian period this is!"

"That's enough!" Ardlyon ordered. "This young person has heard it all before."

"But not from *you*," Penny retorted, "you're always missing at any prize-giving."

"As if that mattered!" he scoffed.

"Don't answer him, Penny. That's not diffidence speaking —it's the green-eyed monster himself!"

Ardlyon had led the laughter at his own expense.

Penny felt ready to soar on a smile, to take wings at a word, to float off on the scent of a gardenia. Silver shone, glass gleamed, champagne sparkled, hothouse flowers shed their delicate intoxication, music rose beguilingly. Festivity prevailed until coffee arrived.

"Why don't you two dance?" Cousin Ida smiled.

Expectantly Penny turned to him—in fact, she almost rose.

To her astonishment, a forbidding look flashed over his face as he glanced at his mother. A look so foreign that for a second Penny scarcely knew him—a look of fear.

Crisply he said: "You know quite well, mother, that I don't dance."

"*Won't* dance!" To Penny's further surprise, Cousin Ida's voice was faintly malicious. "Penny dear, he appears to have taken some sort of Trappist vow not to dance since the war!"

"I'd believe that," Penny winked, "if I hadn't seen him cavorting with Jetty Blake at Georgiana's last spring."

Now he was frowning at Penny. "That was an isolated instance."

"Your one wild oat," Penny said flippantly, and then could have bitten her tongue. She had forgotten how plain Jetty was, and what a poor performer, although that night, certainly, Jetty had yielded her angular frame rhythmically enough to his romantic height and guidance. Too late now, Penny remembered that he had indeed been the last to arrive on that occasion, and the first to go . . . had just waited long enough, in fact, to save Jetty's face.

Lightly Cousin Ida retrieved the situation. "Jetty Blake," she exclaimed, "how very chic—the name, I mean! As one of Lord Tennyson's tiresome ghosts, I really envy her that. So many daughters today are named Susan or Jane, after their grandparents' housemaid—perhaps to commemorate another extinct race! Now, when are you coming north, Penny? Ardlyon works much too hard. That's really what's the matter with him! He must arrange a party soon at Auchteresk. You know how the highlands love a fling!"

The evening had ended in smiles after all.

Penny went home without a dance, yet with a certain excitement. "He was afraid," she remembered.

But in the course of a fortnight, this dubious comfort died.

Ardlyon neither wrote nor telephoned. That promising encounter had gone for nothing. She was once more at a loose end, ready for any distraction.

With Ralph and Sally Townley she had certainly got it in that West End raid.

In the airliner's confining seat, Penny suddenly writhed. Again she relived the entry of the police, when in one horrific instant she had recognized that this was the end—the end of everything—of Ardlyon, Cousin Ida, Auchteresk. That instant, with a sick certainty, had ushered her into a changed world. One which said: this is yours alone now . . . and for keeps. True, the charge against her and the Townleys had later been dismissed, but next day the headlines had been splashed.

It was this unsupportable alteration in the natural order of things that had thrust her into that church at Shepherds Bush. In desperation. And now its peace had gone as well, leaving only a memory of balm. Or was it a clue?

Baffled, Penny felt her brow break into sweat.

"May I have your attention please?"

A voice through a loudspeaker was politely ordering her to fasten her safety belt. She was fast approaching Idlewild Airport.

It was then that Penny took another far-reaching decision. "Mrs. Bell be blowed," she decided, "I'll have a day in New York by myself first."

Already her spirits were rising.

People often had to take another plane. That was why she had been told to telephone the secretary from the airport. Mrs. Bell would not expect her till she telephoned. Everything was dandy—as that American had just exclaimed! First thing tomorrow she would telephone Park Avenue. Meantime, she simply must recover her lost bearings.

There was an hotel she'd heard about—the Barbizon for women. She'd book a room there, right away.

At the Terminal, "Go by Fifth Avenue," she told the cab driver. She might as well start off with a bang!

It was a bright October day, the uproar of traffic muted by towering skyscrapers, yet the delicacy and precision of this unique sky line invited rather than repelled light. It was all a great amazement! Despite the dizzy pinnacles of the Empire State Building and the Rockefeller Center, the heavens had the last word here!

Up and down, Penny drove regardless of dollars. Park Avenue's vista silenced her, Madison allured, while the majesty of Fifth Avenue, dominating its own elegance and glamor, took her breath away. She was spellbound by this dazzling city. That phrase: *the kingdoms of the world* lilted alluringly through her mind, for here was the world's riches, in proud and gay possession, displayed in peerless taste, too!

At the Barbizon, she dismissed her cab, deposited her luggage, and hurried into the street again.

People of all races thronged these pavements. The background was at once so spectacular, and so remote from anything in European experience that she was startled to find her own tongue spoken on all sides!

By six o'clock that evening, when she noticed that the skyscrapers were beginning to tilt towards her, she abruptly knew that this day of exploration had been too strenuous for one so recently in the stratosphere.

Regaining the Barbizon, she found that her ankles had swelled so alarmingly that she could scarcely walk. The doorman was obliged to help her to the elevator.

"Sometimes happens after a long flight," he agreed. "I'll send up a pound of Epsom salts. Put it all in. Don't be frightened."

Lady Penny's bewildering blue eyes opened wider. "Doctor, that would kill a horse!"

It was the doorman's turn to stare. "Get this straight, ma'am. I'm advising on a tub—not a purge."

"Thanks a lot," but as Penny swept swiftly to the fourteenth floor, the unexpected happened.

Softly, silently, persistently, her nose began to bleed.

Gingerly Penny awoke next morning, but mercifully the damn thing had stopped at last, although she now felt weak as water.

The sooner she reached an attentive hostess the better! Pointless to telephone secretary Pratt at this stage. No car would be needed for the airport. She would simply present herself by taxi—after breakfast, of course. She ought to feel better then.

She lay back with a gasp. She was suddenly aware not so much that she was thinking of Ardlyon as the Ardlyon was thinking of her, and with a cold and concentrated fury! This had happened several times since the police case. Hope was dead, of course, but this miserable contact still gave her a dismal satisfaction.

Odd that she should be quailing from a man thousands of miles away! Yet this time his anger held a different element. She was obscurely aware that the Duchess herself was included in his wrath.

As she sat up again, she knew intuitively that Georgiana must have telephoned Auchteresk. Ardlyon was now aware that Penny was in New York.

Pale, and a trifle unsteadily, she arose.

Eleven o'clock was striking as she drove along Park Avenue. The bright, brisk weather of yesterday had changed. Today was sultry with a brazen sky between turret clouds. It was banking up for thunder. For the first time, in a sun glare that was tropical for October she realized that New York shared the latitude of Spain.

Limply, she watched her luggage swung into the entrance of a huge apartment block. The hall was certainly luxurious, but so painstakingly Gothic that Penny was surprised that the doorman was not in armor too.

"Mrs. Cornelia Bell?" he repeated. "No one that name here."

Lady Penny handed him the written address. "Can I get Miss Pratt on the house phone?"

"Miss Pratt!" he exclaimed. "Now you're talking! Apartment D. Go right up."

A Negro in snow white nylon opened the door, ejaculating with delight at the sight of Penny. "Mis' Pratt!" she called, "Mis' Pratt, lady's here!" at the same time flinging wide another door.

Miss Pratt, a short, plump personage of sixty with a pursed mouth, protuberant eyes, and the pink and white skin of a baby, stared in displeasure at the unknown beauty advancing upon her.

Triumphantly, the colored maid had closed the door upon them.

"Sorry I'm a bit late," Penny found herself at once apologizing—such was the force of this new personality, irate of face, tightly corsetted, and as British as Cheltenham or Bath.

"Twenty-four hours late," her hostess enunciated disagreeably. "I am Hester Pratt. I take it that you are Miss Darling."

"Nothing so touching, I'm afraid! I hope there's been no mistake. I am Penelope Ludleigh Tollmache."

In Miss Pratt's memory, the name rang a bell, and not an altogether unsatisfactory one, but at this instant she did not pause to identify it.

"Then you are not the young person introduced by the Duchess of Dunster?"

"Yes, I am. Very much so. I'm related to Georgiana too— I understand you're the secretary. Perhaps you'll be good enough to announce my arrival to Mrs. Bell."

"What nonsense is this?" Miss Pratt's pink cheeks crimsoned. "I expected my secretary yesterday—a vicar's daughter, named Eve Darling, and you turn up to-day for someone else! Regardless of the inconvenience to which I've been put—"

Lady Penny sat down uninvited. "Let's have a look at a telephone directory. Mrs. Bell will soon put us out of our misery."

Fuming, Miss Pratt arose, and pushed a directory forward.

Leafing through this, Penny remarked: "There's probably two of us from the Duchess, and you've got the wrong one."

"Obviously," Miss Pratt retorted unpleasantly. "But that does not explain how such an outrageous mistake could occur nor excuse its gross carelessness."

Penny, however, had begun to enjoy herself. "If you've

never heard of the wrong letter in the right envelope you're not hatched yet! Here's Mrs. Bell's number. What's the betting that she's kidnapped your Darling—and that there's no reply?"

"Reply? Of course there will be a reply. Kindly dial the number yourself. Neuritis has robbed me of the use of my right hand."

But there was no reply, even when an apoplectic Miss Pratt had herself secured and trounced the operator.

"Pipe down," Penny advised. "I'll nip round to Mrs. Bell, and see for myself what's happened. Perhaps I'd better leave my luggage here meantime."

"You certainly will," Miss Pratt exclaimed. "It's out of the question that I'm left unattended this week end—for reasons I shall give you later. If the worse comes to the worst, you'll be better than nothing."

"Optimist," Penny said laconically. "Well, I'm off. Mrs. Bell's address is also Park Avenue, so I shouldn't be long . . ."

She was back in twenty minutes, laughing heartily.

"It's worse than even *you* can guess! The doorman declares that Mrs. Bell flew this week to Florida and an ailing aunt. A young woman arrived at the apartment yesterday, believed to be Lady Penelope Tollmache . . . but clocked-out early today for the week end, with a young man well known to Mrs. Bell. Destination unrevealed, but the worst suspected! Your Darling seems to be a quick worker. The one and only maid left an hour ago. The place is now shut up for the week end. So I'm yours till Monday."

For seconds Miss Pratt was incoherent with indignation.

"What arrant nonsense . . . I never heard such stuff . . . scandalous mismanagement," were a few of the phrases that stuttered from her wrath.

"It's as simple as all that," Penny agreed.

The devil of doubt next seized Miss Pratt. "How do I know this is not a hoax?" she demanded. "You may be an imposter!"

"Here's my passport," Penny flicked it open, "and you can always check up at the Embassy. But now you've begun to bore me. I don't think I *am* yours till Monday—neuritis or not. The Barbizon seems to be calling me home. They couldn't do enough for me there. Epsom salts thrown in regardless—"

"Rubbish!" Miss Pratt came abruptly to her senses. "I need help, and I intend to have it. First of all, there is my mail. Much in arrears. Be good enough to take down these letters."

One letter was all that her temporary secretary achieved. Almost at once her nose began to bleed.

To Miss Pratt's intense annoyance, letter and typewriter were instantly bespattered, and she herself had to hobble first for a key, then for a cold compress—and all for a patient who insisted on lying on the floor . . . an impossible target for her hostess who had not stooped for ten years, and who was privately alarmed by the vivid scarlet dying each proffered towel.

"These airway flights are an abomination," she told her guest testily. "For goodness sake, keep the flow off the carpet—it's valuable. This apartment belongs to a friend of mine who lives in Maine. Fortunately our journey tomorrow is by train."

"*Journey!*" recklessly Penny sat up. "Good Lord, did you say journey?"

Miss Pratt, plump, diminutive on the settee, prodded her down with one foot.

"Of course I said journey. How else can we get there? You don't suppose I've engaged a secretary for fun? It may be months before I can get around alone. My neuritis means constant attention—which must be instantly available. This journey will only take an hour or so—although I understand there is quite a drive at the end of it."

Muffled behind a towel, Penny protested. "Just where are we going?"

"Connecticut, New England—beyond Norwalk. And your annoyance is as nothing to mine. The place has an unpronounceable Indian name, and stands at a confluence of rivers. *A beauty spot* so the travel agent informs me!"

At the ire contained in these three words, Penny's eyes rolled upwards. They were clearly in for complications!

"Can't you postpone Connecticut, Miss Pratt? Wait for your whirlwind worker."

"I can *not*. It is essential that I arrive there tomorrow at latest—or he may again give me the slip."

"He?" Penny rashly lowered the towel.

"I regret, exceedingly, this need for frankness—resent, might be the better word. But as you have to accompany me, you will have to know a certain amount of a most unsavory story. However, I rely on your loyalty. Not one word of this disgraceful matter must ever be repeated."

"For pity's sake, don't rely on me! I'm a regular sieve. And if it's a scandal, I can't get around with it quick enough."

Miss Pratt surveyed her silently, and Miss Pratt silent was even more telling than Miss Pratt vocal. Then tersely she said:

"Not one word will you reveal about my stepbrother's affair. I repeat, it is my intention to face Herbert with the facts tomorrow. You, as my secretary, will accompany me. It is not what I desire, I can assure you. None of this is. And I may add that I find it wholly absurd to address my amanuensis by a title. Further drawbacks are your obvious youth and inexperience. But as it would be incorrect to call you Miss Ludleigh Tollmache, apart from being a ridiculous waste of time, I shall simplify matters by calling you Penelope while you are here—"

"One minute," Lady Penny interrupted: "Does Herbert know we're coming? If he does, it's futile to travel. You'll find he's gone—that's to say if he's not a moron."

"Herbert," Miss Pratt said stonily, "is not aware of my arrival. That is the point of these arrangements. Herbert believes me to be in California. During his visits east, I have always corresponded with him at his New York club. It has only been by chance that I have secured his Connecticut address. Indeed, I was not aware till recently that Herbert *had* a private address!"

"*Hell!*" Penny muttered.

"Ingratitude," Miss Pratt pursued, "is the common lot of the benefactor. But family ingratitude is an abomination—which can at least be dealt with in this case. Herbert—"

"Don't tell me," Penny moaned. "I can't bear more at present. Have a heart, Hester."

Miss Pratt's color mounted to her eyebrows.

"Young woman, persons of your age do not take liberties with people of mine. A Christian name is a familiarity."

"Well," Penny grumbled, "you've gone all matey with mine, and already I feel for Herbert like a brother. But have it your own way, Miss Pratt. Only leave me to bleed alone."

"I'll give you an hour. And if the flow hasn't stopped then, I shall telephone the house doctor. I'm determined to have you on your feet for Connecticut. To malinger will be useless . . ."

Penny, rather ashen, had climbed onto the bed prepared for Miss Darling.

"Count me out till dinner," she announced.

Ungraciously Miss Pratt complied. "But don't be late. We dine at seven-thirty. Downstairs in the restaurant. It will help to harden you off for tomorrow."

Again Penny groaned. "What a taskmaster! You're born to walk upon the faces of the fallen. I bet your middle name is Pharaoh. Do we dress?"

"We do."

Miss Pratt, whose evening attire was a mushroom summer silk worn with a black velvet bolero, was wholly unprepared for her secretary's sensational appearance in the elevator that night. And her stare was again a glare.

Yet no actual fault could be found in Lady Penny's frock, which was, in fact, flawlessly correct for its occasion—a high-necked dinner dress of resida jersey. Cut closely, it was worn with a white jade bracelet. Simplicity itself, but never had beauty seemed so startling. Lady Penny, more ethereal than usual, looked wholly ravishing. Miss Pratt recognized this fact, without for an instant acquiescing with it.

Their progress through the restaurant was triumphal—guests gazed, waiters scurried, and Miss Pratt's annoyance grew. To be conspicuous was her pet aversion. Lady Penny alone appeared oblivious. Lovely as some angel from heaven she simply stated starkly:

"I need a drink."

"Certainly *not!*" Miss Pratt retorted. "After a hemorrhage like that—have you gone crazy? I will not have your blood pressure increased."

"If I don't have a drink at once," Penny said distinctly, "I'll drop down dead. At the Barbizon one can get—" She raised eyes of sea-blue mystery to the waiter.

"One old-fashioned," Miss Pratt ordered sharply. "No, make it two. If anyone needs a pick-me-up, I do."

At their second course, she added. "You'll have to cut the steak for me. My neuritis. *Small* mouthfuls. Not a dog's dinner."

Disgustedly Penny exclaimed. "This steak has barely been introduced to the grill."

"They know I like it rare!" And as the meal mellowed on Miss Pratt she added, "The food is better tonight. And high time too. This meat is succulent. Very sweet and tender."

Penny pushed back her plate. "I think I'll become a vegetarian. I've often thought I might. Oh well, in one way, you're the least of my troubles."

Suspiciously Miss Pratt glanced up. "What do you mean by that?"

"I never wanted to come to New York. It was a sacrifice. At first I felt peace, perfect peace, and all the rest of it. But in under a week I've lost this satisfaction."

"Do your duty," Miss Pratt declared, "and be thankful that things are no worse."

"Look out! You may have to take your own medicine yet."

Loftily Miss Pratt retorted, "I've been doing that ever since I can remember."

"Then the dose may be increased—especially as you've developed a tolerance for it."

"All this pseudo-psychology! I've no patience with such smatterings. God," announced Miss Pratt, "does not work on an incentive basis. He would not be God if He were hoodwinked either by ideals or emotions. Deeds are what He deals with."

Penny nodded. "As you deal with Herbert."

"I shall certainly do my duty there, unpleasant as it may be. To confront this alliance will be enough to confound it. There I am quite confident. I know Herbert. He will sidle out of any difficulty if he gets the chance. But I mean to make matters plain to the woman herself. Once and for all. There can be no repetition."

"But—"

"Allow me to know my own business best."

"Well, I like to know mine too," Penny told her. "For instance: where do we sleep tomorrow night? At Herbert's home from home?"

Miss Pratt, however, was equal to this impudence. Coldly she said: "Levity is lost on me. After the interview we shall drive to a small hotel nearby, of which my agent has given a favorable report. My stepbrother will accompany us. He is twenty years younger than I am, and his future as my business manager depends on it. I have reason to believe he is not a complete fool. Meantime there is nothing more to be said."

"Suits me . . . let's hope it also suits Herbert," and Penny without permission adroitly lit a cigarette.

In a tropical downpour they left Grand Central next day. Humidity was unbearably high, and totally unrelieved by the rain lashing against the speed of their Pullman chair-car.

"Preposterous!" Miss Pratt had briefly denounced the elements, although travelers could still be heard ejaculating on each side. "My, my, and this is the week end we're here to see the foliage!"

These fellow-passengers, having nothing better to do, foolishly spent their time gazing at the breath-taking beauty lounging beside Miss Pratt—blonde hair carelessly tossed, cool eyes, and sleepy smile. The only thing in the girl's favor was that she seemed unaware of her own effect. Everything else about her Miss Pratt deplored, including her flat-heeled strollers. Slipshod, was her senior's verdict. A lazy, lounging girl—and yet race informed her! Frowning, Miss Pratt recognized, then instantly dismissed this fact.

Penny, meantime, was silently congratulating herself that she had cabled the Duchess before she left New York, for Penny never wrote when she could telegraph:

Off to Connecticut for week end with the Pratt, she informed her. *Vicar's daughter took wings in wrong envelope.*

Yes, it had been fun to startle Georgiana with the belated truth!

"Be good enough to open those London papers . . . my neuritis."

Indolently, Penny complied, and at once selected the glossiest for herself.

A somnolent, yet covert silence brooded over the rushing Pullman for an hour, and then Penny sat upright—horribly wide-awake.

For the second time in two days Lord Ardlyon, most reticent of peers, had hit the headlines!

Rumoured Engagement to Miss Daphne Dalrymple ran the tidings. *It will be remembered that Sir Ian Dalrymple's Scottish estate marches with Auchteresk. His daughter, whose dark beauty made her one of the outstanding debutantes of her year, has of late been seen much in public with Lord Ardlyon, and their recent appearance together at the Perth Hunt Ball was an unusually animated one. Well wishers have every reason to believe. . . .*

"What's the matter?" Miss Pratt demanded. "You've gone green again. Put down that paper and lie back! You'll have your nose starting afresh."

Mutely Penny shut her eyes.

Behind closed lids she saw with deplorable distinctness,

Daphne Dalrymple's lustrous brown eyes. A few years older than Penny, as dark as Penny was fair, but—so Lady Penny's detractors claimed—every whit as lovely!

This ghastly news explained, of course, why there had been no follow-through from that dinner at Claridge's.

Abject to argue that this announcement might, after all, prove false. Its shock malignly confirmed it. *This was it!* Hope might have been dead earlier, but some sort of invisible contact had held, like a last lifeline.

Now, everything had gone for if their unseen contact, intuition itself, were false, she was an empty shell. Cracked at that!

But how dare Ardlyon look at her as he had done that night at Claridge's—not once, but repeatedly, renewing their old bond, which dated from first love, from secret adoration?

Fury invaded her suddenly.

She would send him such a cable from Norwalk, as he had never had before!

Yet nothing could be more suitable than that marriage. He and the Dalrymple girl were models of correctitude—peas out of the same pod. She would cable him just that—it would annoy him intensely for he would know precisely what she meant.

Painfully her face flushed—he would also know that she was behaving like a spiteful school girl!

Contemptuously she resisted this cheap temptation.

But cable him she would! A fierce resolve to make her own separation conclusive impelled her. This at least she owed herself—the relief of a clean-cut finish. Pride would prevent her ever saying more than:

Seen announcement in this week's Commentator. Congratulations and goodby.

All at once she was aware that people had risen, up and

down the car. They were gathering in groups, senselessly peering into a sea of rain.

The afternoon had become, alarmingly, as dark as night.

One wag remarked: "What say this train never arrives?" Dutifully his companions laughed.

Half an hour later it did—*but was the last to do so.*

Unknown to themselves, Miss Pratt and Penny were traveling on a day destined to make New England history.

Completely oblivious, Penny was resolving: "I shall send that cable on arrival at Norwalk station if it's the last thing I ever do."

It was, in fact, the last cable to leave Norwalk on Saturday October, 15, 1955.

Ruthlessly Penny rushed to despatch it. Miss Pratt was left vociferating on an empty platform. No porters could be seen. Rain obliterated all but itself—a frightening because a limitless downpour.

Carrying both suitcases, Penny staggered along. Twice she and Miss Pratt took a wrong turning.

Soaked, they reached the deserted entrance. Other passengers had mysteriously vanished. It was like an arrival in a nightmare for the last taxi was now seen to be edging off . . . empty but for the driver.

Both women screamed, and ran at it.

Miss Pratt, unencumbered, was the first to reach it. Clinging to the door with her invalid arm, she vigorously wrenched the handle, and, heedless of the driver's angry protest, fell inside, closely followed by Penny with the luggage.

"What the heck—" he began.

"Once you're out of the town, it's no distance at all," Miss

Pratt lied boldly. "The house is called *Chestnuts,* and it's on River Avenue—the district itself has an Indian name." Briskly she spelled it.

The man was furious. "What d'you think I am—a submarine?"

"No, we believe you to be a man. No man would see a woman stuck. Think of your mother," Miss Pratt adjured him. Unlike the British, all Americans loved their mothers.

The South Norwalk driver proved to be an exception. He accelerated, but with a curse, and the cab lurched out of town. Penny, a tolerable mechanic herself, had never experienced a journey like the next seven miles, as in and out of pools they dipped, along a road that ran by a rushing river, through densely wooded country. At times there seemed to be two rivers in the darkness, or were there three? She only knew for certain that thickets of trees were coming closer and closer.

"All one to you," the driver sneered, "if I get back alive!"

Miss Pratt, innocent as an infant of his aquatic problems, merely said: "It's certainly a very wet night. We shall not ask you to wait more than half an hour at this address before driving us on to the Waterspring Tavern."

This time the driver did not trouble to curse. He merely gave a mirthless bark. "Your funeral, sister, not mine! I'm beating it back to Norwalk now, and I'll be lucky if I'm in before the river's out."

"Then we shall simply telephone the Tavern for another taxi—"

The cab ground to a standstill, in the gloom of one road lamp, beside a derelict open gate.

"Drive to the door," Miss Pratt commanded. "We shall be soaked. This is outrageous."

"For the love of Mike!" Penny pushed her aside. "How

can he possibly turn on a drive that's flowing?" Paying the man, from her own wallet, she recklessly doubled the sum he named, amazed by his forbearance.

Chilled to the bone, they floundered up a path which was now the bed of a rapid stream. In their ears was a new sound, through the darkness, earlier drowned by the car . . . the roaring of many waters, as if they approached some confluence. Over all, came the resounding swish of endless, exhaustless rain.

But lights from a frame house next shone through the criss-cross bower of trees.

Loudly they banged on the door—their summer suits clinging like paper, their hats gummed to their ears, obsessed by one idea only. Shelter.

At the second bang, the door flew back. Expertly they were dragged inside, and the door slammed shut behind them.

Blinking in the brightly lit hall, they found a small, chubby woman beaming at them. She might have been more or less than forty; it scarcely mattered, and neither did her berry-like prettiness. Her amiability was all—the first and last thing about her.

"For goodness sake, you poor souls! I guess you're stormbound . . . come right in to the fire."

"I must apologize . . ." Miss Pratt stopped short. It was the last thing she intended to do.

"Don't say another word . . . Daddy!" their hostess called, "two lovely ladies blown in by the storm."

At this description, Penny guffawed outright to Miss Pratt's intense annoyance, but instantly they were ushered into a large rambling room with window seats, scarlet curtains, walls lined by books, and beakers full of autumn leaves. There was a huge platter of fruit and nuts on an oak dresser, and an atmosphere of bounty which at once suggested Christmas.

By the bright hearth, a white-haired man with mild blue eyes sat quietly smiling. He rose, stick in hand, as they entered, but at once sat down again.

"Come right in," he invited in that deep voice which belongs in richness to certain Americans. "Glad to be of any help. You're very welcome."

But Miss Pratt remained standing. "This visit is not an accident, I regret to say. I have come to see Herbert—Mr. Herbert Houston."

"Herbert?" echoed the cosy little woman. "Isn't that just too bad! Herbert telephoned yesterday he won't be home till Monday. He's gone off in the car with one of our clients to see a property."

Frigidly Miss Pratt retorted: "You are mistaken. The Herbert Houston to whom I refer is of Berkeley, California, and New York."

"Yes, yes, the very same! Now, do sit down, close to the fire . . . Herbert has two agencies, and covers a lot of ground. I'm Mr. Houston's wife, and I know."

"His *wife!*" for a moment Penny thought that Miss Pratt would have a stroke.

"But just call me Chatty," Mrs. Houston was throwing on another log. "Everybody does. Any friends of Herbert's are more than welcome."

"Before we go any further," and Miss Pratt's voice shook with anger, "let me tell you that I am his stepsister, Hester Pratt, and that until this moment I had no idea that Herbert had married."

"Oh, my, oh, my!" sympathetically Mrs. Houston shook her head. "We've been happily married for over a year."

"Why wasn't I informed?"

"I guess Herbert didn't want to upset you. He said he was

waiting for guidance. He felt it wouldn't do to force things. He's
got the kindest heart . . ."

"Sheer cowardice!" Miss Pratt was stuttering with chagrin.

"Come, ma'am," the old gentleman said quietly, "Herbert's way in this was not our way, but then neither were you our
sister. It doesn't do to start advising. That leads to feuding. We
had to leave it to him. My name is Kemble—Frank Kemble. And
this is my daughter—my only child."

"Take off those wet clothes," Mrs. Houston urged. "If
you'll come upstairs, I'll fit you out afresh."

"I absolutely decline," Miss Pratt began, but Penny had
had enough.

"Look at the mess we're making! We're in a pool already.
I'll be thankful to get out of this swim suit!"

"A singularly melodious voice," Mr. Kemble rather oddly
remarked.

"Daddy hears more than most," his daughter fondly exclaimed. "Being blind, you see."

Deeply shocked, Miss Pratt sat down abruptly, but Penny,
stunned, remained standing.

"You'll soon forget about that," Mr. Kemble said mis-
chievously. "Always the nicest compliment anyone can pay me.
Chatty, after you've brought some dry slippers, fetch in the bourbon. Then we must think of supper."

"Out of the question," Miss Pratt said frigidly. "We must
terminate this intrusion. Perhaps you'll allow us to telephone the
Tavern for a car."

Mr. Kemble shook his head. "You don't understand, Miss
Pratt. Friends have already telephoned. For the first time in its
history, the Tavern bridge is down. You were lucky to arrive."

"But that man—our Norwalk driver," Penny interrupted.
"Will he get back?"

"The bridges on that route are still open. Yes, he should get back. But no one else will venture out. You're here till it abates."

"Till what abates?" Miss Pratt expostulated.

Carefully Mr. Kemble said, "Traveling, you wouldn't hear the radio announcement. I'm sorry to be the bearer of bad news. *The floods are out . . .*"

Ten minutes later, clad in an assortment of clothes belonging to Chatty, Herbert, and Mr. Kemble, the visitors sat sipping bourbon with increasing comfort. But in this ease, Penny's heart, burdened by Daphne Dalrymple, sank like a stone. What price now that hint of joy, which like the little waves of a lake said, *coming, coming!*

Flippantly, she struggled to the surface. "What tickles me," and she tossed off her drink, "is that we almost fought the cab driver to bring us here!"

"Humor as well," Mr. Kemble remarked. "Will no one introduce me to our young friend?"

"I beg your pardon," Miss Pratt said for the second time in twenty minutes. "This is Lady Penelope Tollmache."

"And I only wish you could see her, Daddy! She's the most beautiful thing since Helen of Troy!"

Coldly Miss Pratt cut in: "Lady Penelope is a relative of the Duchess of Dunster. Unluckily for her, the Duchess confused two introductions and Lady Penelope arrived yesterday instead of the secretary I expected. A most regrettable error for all concerned!"

Mr. Kemble chuckled. "Her Grace presents—the other person! Yet who knows? It may prove to be the right one after all. In fact, it must be the right one, as this is destiny. May I know the name of your secretary, Miss Pratt. The one who was expected?"

"Miss Eve Darling, a clergyman's daughter."

"Miss Eve Darling," he repeated, almost lovingly. "Now what do you think has happened to her?"

"She arrived safely, at the house of an absent millionairess," Penny told him, "and vanished at once with a fine young man!"

Mr. Kemble laughed, "While you make-do with a fogey aged seventy-five? There must be some sound reason for such a poor exchange. Well, well, a mistake had to get you here, yet nothing could prevent it. All the time, of course, you've been *coming, coming . . .*"

"Say that again," Penny said in a strangled voice.

"All this time you've been coming, coming, dear pilgrim."

To Miss Pratt's astonishment, the old gentleman was looking at Penny as if he saw her distinctly, knew her quite well.

"I think," the girl was saying slowly, "that I have come to the right address after all, Mr. Kemble. Quite a number of questions I'd like to ask you. A great deal I want to know."

"And so you shall," he said soothingly. "Rest for the present. There will be plenty of time."

Stiffly Miss Pratt said. "I can only repeat my regrets— that we are adding to your anxieties, Mr. Kemble, and possibly depleting your stores."

"Don't give that another thought. Sorry you had to be here for this crisis, but glad to have you with us for every other reason. Lady Penelope, too."

The famous American hospitality, Penny noted. No fuss, an immediate acceptance of the situation, all with a simplicity that was grace.

"I'm just so sorry," Chatty confessed, "that you two lovely people will have to share our only guest room. Twin beds, of course—and you do have your own bathroom. Perhaps Miss Pratt would like to unpack first, while I get supper?"

Privately shattered, Penny had gone upstairs when Miss Pratt came down. Bad enough to have to live with the Pratt, but she really drew the line to sharing this small homely bedroom with her!

Morosely, she went into the bathroom where Miss Pratt had earlier staked her claim. In the first of two tumblers, Miss Pratt's nasal syringe stood sentinel, with a traveling teaspoon that dispensed Miss Pratt's morning salts. The other glass bristled with a selection of denture brushes—sturdy implements with gray, bushy heads which Janus-like faced both ways. Penny had never seen their like before, and "loathsome" was her verdict. Miss Pratt's black and white sponge bag swung from the razor hook. Miss Pratt's out-sized sponge bulged from the bath. Miss Pratt's red rubber shower cap crowned the peg allotted to Penny's towel, while, on the back of the door, in silent but ultimate triumph, Miss Pratt's purple dressing gown held the pass! Penny was not only defeated, she was obliterated.

Dear Lord, she muttered, aren't you going a little too far with this?

Yet supper was unexpectedly cheerful. Chatty proved an accomplished cook—Herbert was clearly in clover! Miss Pratt, glaring at Penny and Mrs. Houston by turn, chatted politely enough with Mr. Kemble, who had traveled quite as widely as herself. Such was the mollifying influence of good food, perfectly prepared and attractively served, that soon their elderly exchanges took on the pleasant nature of memories shared.

For a little, flood water rushing sibilantly off the roof was forgotten and shortly, Chatty had settled them down to a television comedian. "Daddy enjoys his back-chat—no, no, I always wash up alone."

Surprisingly quickly, this capable treasure rejoined her party of three at the illumined screen. "Glad I'm in time for the news," she chirruped.

And then it happened—in the flash of an eye—a devastating explosion which rocked the house and blotted out all light.

Stunned, they sat like corpses in pitch darkness.

Then Chatty's voice reached them, and Penny saw a battery torch gleam.

"Hello there . . . bless you! That was more than our main fuse. Something must have happened to the town dynamo. The road lights have gone too. Don't move till I light candles. Everything will soon be dandy."

"Chatty," her father's voice came quickly, "did you manage to draw any water from the artesian?"

"Before supper. Every container's full."

"Good for you," he purred. "Now, friends, this is something of a crisis, and I can't conceal it. We shall have to take a few precautions from the word go! No water can be drawn in the house now. No drinking, washing, or flushing the toilet. It's also forbidden to touch any electric light switch. I needn't tell you that all this water around is now liable to be electrically charged. But things are better than they might be, for there's an oil stove we can cook on when, and if, the fuel for the fire is exhausted. And we're well supplied with stores."

"But, Daddy, I've just realized—the radio's electric too. We can't get any news. We won't know how . . . how . . ."

"How bad it is!" he laughed cheerfully. "Yes, we will. There's Herbert's battery-set in the hall. Bring it in right away, and it'll be ready for tomorrow. But bed now while we're warm, as there's no knowing how long this chimney will continue to draw."

Upstairs, in the gloom, one candle revealed that Miss Pratt's carefully staked claims in the bathroom were now annulled. Calamity had taken care of these! Abstractedly, both undressed, and Penny, exhausted, fell asleep instantly.

Waking next morning, she discovered Miss Pratt in the act of relighting the candle in their darkness—the tropical deluge still gushing over the house.

"Did you sleep?" Penny asked.

"Intermittently."

"I think I must have done so, too." Penny fumbled for conviction.

"You have slept profoundly," Miss Pratt retorted.

"Did I snore?"

"I cannot say you snored," Miss Pratt said resentfully, "but you have slept noisily. Calling out repeatedly about that place in Scotland—what's its name . . . Auchteresk."

"Sorry, must have been maddening. What's the time?"

"Eight o'clock. Mr. Kemble and his daughter are both moving around."

"All right, I'll get up and out of the way. Deathly cold, isn't it?"

"Yes," Miss Pratt grudgingly agreed.

In a twilight that was now day in this changed world, Penny got into her clothes, grumbling. Her teeth were chattering with more than chill, but deliberately she ignored the ceaseless rushing of unseen water around them. This house, in its dense thicket of trees, was like a bird's nest lost in a torrent. Stumbling into the corridor, she hesitated for a second.

As she did so, the house—very slightly, in a sly, stealthy way—swayed beneath her.

Instantly she opened the bedroom door again. "Did you feel that?"

"No, I did *not!*" Miss Pratt was sitting bolt upright with an outraged expression. "You will oblige me by remaining silent on this subject downstairs."

"Even if they remark on it?"

"Precisely."

A reluctant admiration flickered across Penny's face. "Okay," she said heavily.

In the lounge, by candle light, Chatty was on her knees beside the log fire. Obviously there had been trouble in making the chimney draw—the pleasant room was rather smokey. But now a comforting glow shone from the hearth, and Mr. Kemble was smiling cheerfully from his own perpetual darkness.

"Breakfast first," Chatty promised, "then the news!" She bustled off.

Silently, Penny sat down.

"Scared?" Mr. Kemble inquired humorously, as if the question were itself a joke.

She gave a short laugh. "On and off. But I don't believe that Miss Pratt is."

"No, poor dear," he said, "she's come to terms with everything already—except joy."

Penny frowned. Rather defiantly she said, "Of course I realized from the start that you had a sixth sense, that you knew all about us already."

"When did things begin to go wrong for you?"

"When they first seemed to go right. But after a ghastly mistake I'd made—I heard a remarkable sermon. That saved me. For a little I thought I'd found heaven on earth . . . but only for a little."

He nodded. "Another frontier incident, then fresh trouble. Your experience had to be sustained, or you were not free."

"Of course—but how? I thought I'd crossed the border. In fact, I know I had."

He laughed. "Agreed. But you didn't remain at peace, did you?"

"You mean it was really a kind of trespass? Well, perhaps it was. But nothing else has mattered since. And I can't get back. To that security, I mean."

Impatiently, she walked across to the streaming window, impenetrably gray as the bottom of a pond. "To me the shocking thing about this flood is that there's that other existence—really almost heavenly. And that there's this as well, the feeling that God's not in this outer upheaval at all."

"The wind, the earthquake, and the fire," Mr. Kemble quoted easily, "and God was not in any of them! But, don't forget, will you, that Christ is Lord of the elemental world, as well as all else."

"I hear what you say, of course, but I'm back where I was before I believed."

"With this difference—that now you're yearning for that lost certainty, which means you're really on your way to it."

Penny turned and stared at him. "You think so?"

"I know so! Now you're down to bedrock, and though that's as narrow and humbling as a grave, it's the only exit that is truly an entrance."

Chatty, followed by Miss Pratt, came briskly into the room, and breakfast was eaten round the fire.

"A great deal can be done with a helicopter," Miss Pratt affirmed, "it is simply a matter of time."

"In a thicket? What a hope!" Penny scoffed.

"Kindly keep your defeatist views to yourself. You have newly arrived in this country, or you would know that it is fully organized for every emergency."

Tactfully Chatty turned on the battery set, and they found themselves listening to the first of those bulletins that were henceforth to punctuate their hours.

An urgent American voice was announcing: " 'Deep disaster now threatens Connecticut . . . Havoc is wide in Danbury, Stamford, and Norwalk areas . . . Blast cuts power. Rains increasing in violence all night have turned rivers and streams into raging floods. Houses have capsized, bridges are washed away, roads are undermined. Householders are even now being rescued from their roofs, or from tree tops by helicopters . . . Helicopters have also rescued eighty-three passengers on the stranded 7:28 train from New York, after a twelve hour marooning . . . On the collapse of the roadbed, the New Haven freight has been wrecked. Not a train will run today throughout New England. The National Guard has been alerted . . . We are interrupting this bulletin to make a special announcement in sixty seconds.' "

In an uneasy silence, Miss Pratt could be heard announcing with every sign of satisfaction: "I call that something like service!" Restless and resigned by turn, Penny's gaze remained withdrawn. Solicitously Chatty eased the logs in their thickening smoke. Mr. Kemble amiably waited.

Then the announcement came:

"Governor Ribicoff has declared a state of emergency in Connecticut. He has arrived by National plane at 10:15 this morning. He has also appealed to the White House for emergency funds as rising water has already left 4,130 families homeless; isolated scores of communities; and brought death to others."

Slickly Mr. Kemble turned the set off. To Penny's further astonishment, he gave a low chuckling laugh.

"Well, my dears," he said, "here it is! And here we are together for it. I guess it does us all good, once in a while, to face up to facts."

Rather stupidly they stared at him, and then slowly smiled. Catastrophe was in no way lessened, but in contact with his calm, they too achieved sanctuary—for a second.

Penny swallowed, then nodded. "I know what you mean. The thing's appalling, but in its own way, it's superb."

Miss Pratt glanced at her with disgust. Distinctly she said: "I've suspected it before, but now I know. *You are completely unhinged!*"

Thereafter, there were hours that dragged like years, minutes that passed like hours. Already they seemed to have been a lifetime in this house which knew no morning, but merely passed into a twilight that prefaced further darkness.

It was at one such moment that Penny was suddenly aware of the Duchess thinking frantically about her. Those cables had been received! Then Georgiana was blotted out by a more urgent image—that of Ardlyon, listening to the latest radio news. So vivid was this impression of him that from that instant Daphne Dalrymple ceased to weigh on Penny's heart.

All over the world, Connecticut suspense was mounting.

Yet there were also friendly periods with Mr. Kemble and Chatty when time eased off, although when Penny next looked at her watch, minutes only had gone. She was still stationary in this rushing gloom.

All at once the ruined telephone rang clearly!

Aghast, each started to their feet. Chatty was the first to seize the silent receiver.

"I'm sure it's Herbert!" she cried, almost in tears. "The poor boy must be frantic about us. If anyone can get through, it will be Herbert!"

"Herbert—tush!" Miss Pratt had recovered. "It's typical of him—yes, typical, to escape all this unpleasantness!"

The telephone did not ring again.

Before noon, the first helicopter could be heard whirring around their tree tops. Then, like all subsequent helicopters, its furore persisting for a period, slowly, almost reluctantly it faded out.

Water alone continued to gush monotonously.

At two o'clock, gloom lessened through the windows. A break in the cloud blanket revealed that final inundation was within five feet of the house.

For the first time Chatty was unnerved. "Oh, Daddy, what are we going to do? Already the cellars are full."

"Yes, yes," he soothed her, "but you know as well as I do that the cellar doors are open, that it's running freely down the drive."

"Mebbe, but think of the Riddocks, and old Mrs. Stacey and Miss Madison, if this has happened to us! Their homes stand much lower."

"I know, I know! But they're in the open. They'll all have been taken off by now."

So it went on, each taking refuge in the personal idiosyncrasy that adds interest, annoyance, or distraction to crisis. So often did Miss Pratt affirm her faith in American efficiency that even Mr. Kemble sighed. Religiously Penny debunked every pious hope that Miss Pratt assiduously and Chatty genially shared.

Periodically, Miss Pratt and Penny withdrew to their bedroom for a little.

Irascibly Miss Pratt admitted, "I must say that that woman is showing up very well. But her ridiculous habit of adding, 'bless you' to each remark is nauseating."

"M'yes," Penny agreed, "it's tacked on like an extra breath. But look out! All that kindness means energy. It's not a virtue with them. They're bursting with vitality. They really mean it. We think we're hard boiled, but I suspect we're only tired. They simply cannot credit our British snubs. They'll give us the benefit of the doubt till kingdom come. And soon we won't be able to do without their amiability. They're like a drug. Insidious."

"Rubbish," Miss Pratt stumped downstairs again.

"A little music?" Mr. Kemble was suggesting. "There's not much now we can offer in the way of entertainment, but we have a number of fine records and this old turntable."

Miss Pratt, luckily, liked music. It was almost the only thing she did like. But it had to be music of a specific sort, otherwise she refused to recognize its claim. Seated at a bandstand, she welcomed a robust march or a rousing chorus. And if she could beat time to this, she enjoyed the occasion still more.

"A nice march or a Viennese waltz is always welcome," she announced, "but I warn you I detest all modern makeshifts."

"Perhaps Lady Penny will help us to pick out something suitable." Mr. Kemble said. *"Sancta Musica!"* he added absently, as if invoking unseen help.

"As I detest marches," Penny informed them, "and Viennese waltzes still more, we'll have turn about."

To Miss Pratt's surprise and boredom, Lady Penny's tastes

proved to be classical! But now that the older woman had to sit out Bach and Beethoven, through the interminable hours of that weary day, she began to detect patches of pleasure in the masters' wilderness. Tantalizing oases. Later, Miss Pratt actually discovered, here and there, a thread of continuity, some order in their chaos. At this, a spurt of enthusiasm enlivened her. She had almost a sense of personal accomplishment! Then, quite quickly, she knew nothing but exhaustion.

Alone with Penny for a little, Miss Pratt irritably ordered her to put Handel aside.

"But you seemed to like my choice latterly. Oh, well, here you are!"

This time Lehar failed to charm.

Miss Pratt ordained his end too. "You've simply unsettled me for both sorts."

"No," Penny said with a flicker of interest, "you're developing. It's really rather extraordinary."

Such presumption was incredible. "I am *what?*"

"Maturing. In vulgar idiom: the classical bug's bitten you. Quicker than it gets most people. You're probably naturally musical if your taste had not been ruined."

But for once impertinence failed to register. Miss Pratt was arrested by Penny's first sentence.

If this were true, perhaps she had at last found a cure for her general malaise, the ennui which had for years afflicted her like a creeping disease. Music might prove a new interest. Mr. Kemble was older than she was, and stone blind, yet obviously he did not suffer from her own increasing boredom. Music might prove the very thing for her, the interest she needed. If she were spared, she'd go further with this matter.

Abruptly her attention flagged. Her pallor increased. *If she were spared—*

"After you've had a meal," Penny prophesied, "you'll be as keen as mustard for more of the unutterable."

But the next news bulletin eclipsed all but itself.

"Today parts of Connecticut look like a mass of boiling water, as seen from helicopters fiercely buffeted . . . In Norwalk the river has torn into the heart of the city, and swept down the main street, crumbled the town's largest buildings, ripped up four bridges and knocked out the electrical supply. Northern New England is virtually isolated today except by air . . . Sewage disposal plant is seriously damaged and emergency health measures are being taken . . . The people to report, where possible, for innoculation . . . A seven o'clock curfew is now declared. The latest weather report is that wind is coming up."

It came.

In blacker, more blinding draughts of water—that was the only change. In a sense, they scarcely noticed the wind. Water was the obsession. They no longer thought of it as rain.

If it kept on flooding?

Hot soup, at this stage, hurriedly postponed the implication of this threat. Surprisingly good soup too!

Then Mr. Kemble asked Penny to put on another record.

At this crisis, had anyone told Miss Pratt that within the next half hour, despite worsening conditions, she would know the joy of a lifetime, she would, incredulously, have scoffed.

But with the first bars of this particular record, it happened.

Calm imposed its own spaciousness. She was sweet-and-twenty again, with her life and Christian Thord before her. He was smiling that first smile to her, for, from the start everything had gone right for them. Everyone had approved of her Norwegian geologist. Except Mamma, who found him too old at thirty for her only daughter. Yet Christian merely laughed when

Hester launched forth on the subject of Mamma! With Christian all Hester's tensions eased, which gave her new-found freedom. And he brought her fascinating gifts, that she marveled over in his absence: a chambered nautilus; a conch shell; a fossilized ammonite. As he placed the last in her small pretty hands he said: "My dear heart, how easily you carry your seventy-seven million years!" Cheerfully she retorted: "But of course—now I have forgotten time!"

Later that day, crossing the street, he had looked up at her window, and waved. Her bridgroom of tomorrow.

And then the speeding roadster cut him down . . .

With surprising swiftness Hester Pratt had stiffened into dictatorial spinsterhood.

Until this moment in the flood disaster, when unknown music of a peculiar nature sounded and it was spring again, the first grass cut around a dream house, that was strange yet familiar, as some honorable award. Her home and Christian's, as they shared this harmony. This was their tomorrow, but now it was today. Why had she never guessed that present happiness was coexistent with past joy? The years that she had lost when they might have been together thus! But all error was temporal. Within this present they were one forever.

Faster and faster flew the music—neighbors and friends were come with country fiddlers to this unseen wedding. Only the eldest sounded a warning note, lost in the festivity. Yet this dark figure was no longer fate, but an interpreter revealing as mortal myth, terror, dismay, suffering, and death. Iron, bronze and stone age, so it had always been. But now no longer! With his last smile, which was also his first, she could hear Christian say again: "My dear heart, how lightly you carry your seventy-seven million years!"

Lady Penny lifted the record off.

Hoarsely Miss Pratt said: "What is it called?"

"Appalacian Spring," Mr. Kemble told her. "The composer Aaron Copland has described it as springtime on a Pennsylvania farm, where the bride-to-be and her future husband are discovered in tenderness and passion. A revivalist and his flock arrive, and the lovers are reminded of the strange and terrible aspects of human fate. But in the end, the couple are left quiet and strong in their new home."

"It will seem incredible to you," Miss Pratt said, in the voice of a woman who has not sopken for forty years, "but, as I listened, I lived through that identical story, scene by scene, exactly as you describe."

"I *told* you that you were naturally musical," Penny began, and then stopped short.

Miss Pratt was shaking her head with an altered authority.

"More than music went to my experience," she replied. "Nevertheless, I am indebted to you all."

"Sancta Musica!" Mr. Kemble murmured benignly, as if saluting space.

"And I'm just so sorry to tell you," Chatty hurried downstairs, "but we're running out of candles. As a housewife, you'll think I'm the world's worst! I guess I've been regulated too long by that little old electric switch! Do you two lovely people think that you can manage in your bedroom with yesterday's stump? We have to think ahead in case the rain goes on."

Anxiety on Chatty's cheerful face was like age before its time and Penny glanced away.

Tonight it was Miss Pratt who fell asleep, as her head touched the pillow.

The last news bulletin had stunned Penny. *More Rain.*

Yet it had earlier been declared, by radio, that more rain would mean the end.

Then, exhausted, Penny too dropped off . . . and sleeping, dreamed.

Dreamed of Claridge's again. Cousin Ida was in the background, but Ardlyon and Penny were real as they had never been in life. They had only to smile at one another to read the other's thought.

"Breathlessly beautiful!" he repeated in the dream, but now with such a difference! Silver shone, glass gleamed, flowers shed their perfume, music rose beguilingly. Festivity prevailed— and then he said with rather a curious emphasis, "Will you dance the last waltz with me?"

Eagerly she arose, when in the dream Ardlyon himself altered before her eyes! He was dressed for action of a very different sort. In scarlet tunic and bearskin, he stood there at attention, his drawn sword in his hand—an officer on guard.

Yet with the same strange emphasis he repeated: "Will you dance the last waltz with me?"

"Always!" she exclaimed, and at this curious set distance, they continued to confront one another, while the music waltzed without them. Yet never had they been closer, as, exquisitely, endlessly the waltz encircled both. "Always," she repeated, and in her anxiety to reassure him, she suddenly awoke.

Something terrible was about to happen to Ardlyon— no, to herself!

Escape by sleep from flood had always this dire awakening—insistent and relentless rain!

Raising herself on her elbow, she listened, and now, in the darkness the water from below clucked and sucked more busily round the little house.

Her idiotic heart had begun to beat too quickly—she, who had always taken her physical courage for granted!

There too she had been mistaken.

Abruptly she sat up in bed, for, to the sound of that incessant downpour, came a reminder, linked with earlier calm, of little waves of joy that had said *coming, coming.*

Little waves . . . in a cold sweat she lay down again.

Yet there was Miss Pratt tonight, peacefully asleep beside her! Something had happened to Hester during *Appalacian Spring.* The flood scarcely seemed to matter to her now. Fear, not death, was clearly the last enemy, as had been often said.

Outside now, Penny could again hear the advancing and retreating helicopter, only a degree less ghoulish than that fading fog siren.

And here they were, slowly submerging in their bird's nest of a house! She wondered what Ardlyon would say if the worse came to the worst. He'd probably think it was the only dignified thing she'd ever done—going west without a word! No, that wasn't fair. He'd be appalled, and she knew it, knew it when it was too late—

Again she sat up. This awakening was the most frightful thing that had ever happened to her.

She must pray. Pray for what? Escape? Others had not escaped, why should she? All the same, she must pray—it was the last thing left.

What could she say in this exhaustion?

"Our Father . . ." she began dumbly, obediently. Again and again she repeated these two words. They were all she could manage.

After a time, sitting upright on the shrouded bed, the quilt around her, she grew drowsy, but tenaciously she clung to the two words, and, in a little while, found to her astonishment that drowsiness had passed and that the words were now supporting her. More slowly, more clearly she told them. Tranquilly, the prayer took over, and in the gloom the rushing water became of lesser note. Shortly, in some mysterious way, the prayer achieved an athlete's second-wind for her. It was now effortless. A quiet, continuous solace.

Downstairs, the grandfather clock struck four in the morning.

All at once, Penny was startled by a silence unknown for days.—

The rain, contrary to prophecy, decreased, dwindled, ceased.

Almost to that instant, the bedroom window sprang into moist, bright light from the road lamp. Engineers at headquarters, working night and day, had achieved another miracle. Miss Pratt's faith in American efficiency was brilliantly justified!

Yet to Penny, lapped by the security of her prayer, safety itself was, for the moment, of secondary importance—a fact that ever after was to remain the wonder of her life.

And at six o'clock that morning, over the scene of desolation, four words were flashing above, beyond the tidings that rivers recede, rains stop, thousands are homeless, millions of dollars are lost . . . four words that in funereal black stared from New York's posters one hour later: THE WORST IS OVER.

But by nightfall next day, the London papers held more frivolous headlines on the subject: *Peer flies the Atlantic . . . Ardlyon to Bring Lady Penny Back . . . Delighted Dowager Anticipates Early Wedding . . . Rejoicings at Auchteresk.*

Ardlyon himself, seated impatiently on a B.O.A.C. airliner that was mincing along at the imperceptible speed of 325 miles an hour, reflected grimly enough that if many waters cannot quench love, they can amazingly clarify it!

Not for the first time had Penny gone too far, but assuredly for the last! This time she was coming home—for good. Yes, by heaven.

Joseph

Joseph

I am a novelist first and last.

From the moment that I saw the man I knew there was a story there.

We were the only men in a first-class smoking compartment on the 8:40 boat train from Dover. It was a windy October night. The crossing had been unpleasant and prolonged. And my unknown companion had fallen asleep opposite, on our return from the dining car.

He was a thick-set man approaching middle age, with an undistinguished face. At dinner I noticed that his expression was intelligent, but something in the thrust of his shoulders and sunburned hands suggested one who had labored with his body, rather than his head. Yet his clothes were good. In an unostentatious way they were remarkably good. I could not place the man. His luggage, too, was old and of the best quality. Now, if it had been new—

As I studied him asleep there in the corner, I saw that he was smiling. Smiling seraphically. And this expression on his commonplace face appealed to my sense of the ludicrous. Another might have glanced away, in fear of awakening him, but I repeat I am a novelist first and last. The man piqued my curiosity. Moreover, I had finished reading my newspaper. I felt that he had slept long enough. I wondered what his thoughts were, and found myself wishing that I could read them.

As I watched him, it seemed almost as if we were in some sort of contact, for after a time the smile faded, his mouth moved, he began to mutter, and a look of deep distress grooved itself round his lips. A few drops of sweat rose on his brow.

I decided to awaken him.

He came out of his sleep with a violent start, but, to my surprise, with a look of tender pleasure.

"Good lord, that's a queer thing!" he exclaimed, his blunt hands fumbling with his tie and collar.

"You have had an agreeable dream?" I suggested.

"Agreeable?" emphasis appeared to fail him. "I've had the most extraordinary dream I've ever had! And, mind you, I dream a lot." He leaned forward impulsively. "In fact, extraordinary isn't the word. I've just dreamed a complete book!"

I was almost as astonished as he was. "A writer, by any chance?" but my inquiry was purely conventional.

"Great scot, no! That's what makes it so amazing. I've dreamed a complete book. From beginning to end. And what makes it stranger still, it was a book of three short stories. I can tell you every word, but first I must write down a name before I forget." He began feeling hurriedly in his pocket for paper. He also retrieved a stump of pencil. I noticed that his fingers were shaking as he wrote down some words.

"That's it!" he gave a sigh of relief, and then rather a shamefaced laugh. "You must think my behavior a bit odd."

"Not at all. I am a novelist myself. And your dream interests me. Had the book a name, by any chance?"

"No," he said, "no I can't remember the name, or the author," he began to look worried. "That's funny, you know. Already it's slipping away from me. But it was a complete book. And I know it was by a good author. A peg above the stuff I generally amuse myself with—really, you know, a good writer!" He was pathetically anxious to rub this in. I feared I was about to be bored.

I held out my cigarette case. "Quite," I assured him. "A master of his craft, no doubt."

"That's it!" His expression was eager, and for the first time I noticed one peculiarity of his particularly uninspiring face. The eyes were set remarkably far apart, and of the pale, bright blue you find in Celtic people. "The author was a master of his craft. Literature isn't in my line, as a rule, but I can remember whole pages, whole sentences!"

Once more, in his excitement, he showed signs of becoming inarticulate.

"But what happened, man?" I urged less now from interest, than impatience. "If the book was so vivid, surely it left you with more than a string of adjectives . . . some outline or other?"

"The *second* story," he began, with emphasis, "made a deep impression. It was the story of a snob. Quite an ordinary sort of chap he was, just like you or me. Nobody would have suspected it of him. I didn't myself till the end of the story. And it gave me a nasty feeling, I don't mind telling you. Yet there's nothing criminal in being a snob, is there?"

"I should say not. But what did the fellow do? How did he reveal himself?"

"Well you know, that was curious too!" My companion leaned forward, his hands loosely knotted between his knees. "He fell in love with a girl a cut above him. At least, although she wasn't rich—and he was, by this time—she came of older stock. She lived in a house with a funny name. The one I've just written down here. And her name was Kate. He didn't like this name, for it didn't suit her. It was too sensible. She was the lovely dreamy sort. And he didn't like Kate for her, any more than anyone would have."

"He should have called her Catherine," I remarked, with barely concealed irony.

He looked up quickly, and I saw that I had gone too far. "I have a sentiment for the name," I improvised smoothly. "It is my wife's."

"Kate?"

"No, of course not. Catherine—but do go on with your story. What was the name of the house?"

"I can't pronounce it. I think its Gaelic. And although I'm a Scot, I don't know Gaelic. That's why I wrote it down. I saw every letter quite distinctly. And the name had a lot to do with the story. It was one reason why he married her. And yet he was always chipping her about it and the place—"

"Place?" I enquired a little whimsically.

"Yes, it was one of those. A lot of ground round it. And a lodge. But all gone to rack and ruin," he shook his head, and in a voice of extreme commiseration added, "even the drains."

"Dear me!" I murmured.

"Yes. And when he used to chip her about the place, she never could understand it. She grew quieter and quieter. 'Strange as it may seem'—" He held up a warning finger, and I realized he was quoting from his masterpiece, " 'Strange as it may seem, she was often near to tears.' "

"I think I can understand that," I remarked. "Go on."

"She was a lovely creature," he said reminiscently. "The author made you feel that. There was a feeling about her like the —like the—"

"Breath of dawn?" I suggested, taking the edge off my ennui with impudence.

"That's right!" he said gratefully. "She was like the dawn. Unspoiled. Here's the name of the place. You see, it's written in three words with hyphens between."

I took the paper from him, and read this inscription: Ti-Ekat-Ecued.

"Seems rather Eastern," I remarked.

"No," he said with conviction. "I remember that much. It was Welsh or Gaelic, a language that belongs to this country. You don't know Gaelic, do you?"

"A few words only. And these are certainly not among them. But there are several distinguished Celtic societies that might help you, of course, in your researches."

He took back the paper rather sadly. "I can't help feeling it's a clue, you know!" and he attempted to read it aloud. "Ti-Ekat-Ecued."

My interest was suddenly aroused. I held out my hand for the paper. "I wonder if it means anything spelled backwards."

"Backwards?"

"Yes—you've surely taken a walk in the suburbs, at one time or another? Well, then, you must often have seen names as exotic as this painted on door or gate. Generally shorter ones, I admit. But if you turn some of those suburban names round, you invariably discover them to be the names of the proud owner's wife or mother. Now, let me see . . . no, thanks, I have my pen. Yes, I am right. Your name makes sense, my dear sir. But not the sense you suppose. Your heroine lived in a house called 'Deuce-take-it.' "

He studied the paper with a look of incredulity. "But that's nonsense! How could anyone live in a house called 'Deuce-take-it.' "

"I'm sure I don't know," I shrugged my shoulders to suggest that a change of topic was indicated. "Your heroine apparently managed it. Of course there may have been the devil to pay there!"

At those words he suddenly sat bolt upright. "But of course!" he almost shouted. "That was the reason. The whole thing's come back to me now. There *was* the very devil to pay."

I glanced at my watch a trifle deliberately. "I think you said there was another story?"

"Two. But I can't remember a thing about the first in the book now. Perhaps because I read it first."

"Perhaps!" I interrupted.

"But the *last* story," and now he leaned forward again, "made an extraordinary impression on me—extraordinary. I can remember more sentences out of that story than the other. And there was one scene I shall never forget. There was a woman—she wasn't in black but I knew at once that she was in deep mourning—you know how you do in a dream. There had been a funeral that afternoon, and there was going to be another in three days. There was a man standing near the woman in the room but he wasn't important. He didn't really matter. It was the woman who did, and she stood staring at a white chrysanthemum at her feet. It wasn't up to much, as flowers go, a bit—" he fumbled.

"Papery?" I suggested mechanically.

"That's right. Papery. The very word I was feeling for. And she stood staring at it with her great frightened eyes—"

But by this time I could bear no more. "My good sir," I

said firmly. "I think I can explain your dream. As you slept you relived some forgotten book, read in your youth."

"No!" he exclaimed with heat, "and that much I can prove! *I was a great deal older when I read that book in the dream than I am now!*"

"Indeed?" I lit another cigarette. "You were wearing perhaps a long white beard to match the flower?"

But this time my irony left him unscathed, he was completely absorbed in his half-baked tale. "No!" he repeated, and as the smoke of my cigarette cleared, I noticed an expression half shy, half proud on his face. "But I know I was older, more up in those things, if you get me, than I am now, for as I read the story one sentence didn't ring true. Even though it was literature. And I spotted it—in a way I couldn't have done *before* the dream. You see, I'd been sailing along with this author in fine style, seeing eye to eye with him in everything, and all at once he let me down. The poor attach a lot of importance to flowers at funerals. And there had been some difficulty over those chrysanthemums. But one had been saved for the living woman. Then all at once the author made this woman stoop and steal it. Now I know that that woman could never have stolen anything. And anyway never that flower for that was the queer thing about it. That one flower had been given back to her."

"Indeed!" I intoned.

"Yes," he nodded, and then paused. "Funny, isn't it, the way funerals have of happening in raw weather. I myself," and he stared at the ground for a moment, "have buried my nearest and dearest."

In spite of the irrelevance of this remark, his tone had the restraint of an authentic and exhaustless grief, and would have been quite impressive had it not been for the banality of the words themselves.

"Well, as I was saying, the end was particularly fine, for in the last sentence of the book, the man and woman were left confronting each other—that was the very word the author used. 'Confronting' "—again he raised his finger to indicate quotation marks. " 'A man and wife confronting each other—a wife who would remain his for ever.' " He stopped short, the last of his curious excitement draining from him. "I'm sure," he said almost apologetically, "I don't know why that seemed so significant but it did, *'a wife who would remain his forever.'* "

I remained, with determination, silent.

"I'm sure," he began again, "you've been very patient. Now, that was a queer thing you know, that about those house names! I was born in a slum, and reared in a suburb—just the sort you spoke of—and I never once tumbled to some of those outlandish names." His pale eyes were watching me with interest, an interest I no longer reciprocated.

"It's part of my job," I replied noncommittally, "to be observant."

"There's more to your job than that," he said heartily. "You needn't tell me! I'm observant myself. But I couldn't write a book."

"Oh, don't say that!" I murmured with elaborate politeness, for by this time I could see the lights of the city flashing along the line in the darkness, and knew that relief was at hand. "You've just dreamed one. Why not get that out of your system by writing it next time."

"I?" he looked incredulous, and yet at the same time impressed by the idea. For a moment I began, privately, to question his sanity.

"But I can't remember the name of the book!" he spoke as if this difficulty were insuperable.

"Invent one then. Call it *Author Unknown.*"

He shook his head impatiently. "I've forgotten too much."

"Fill in the gaps by running the stories together then!" I suggested brazenly, stretching my cramped limbs.

At these words, once again he stared at me strangely, and I saw now that his excitement had left him very pale.

"But that is exactly what did happen," he protested. "You keep bringing it back to me. There *was* a link between the stories. The first was his story, the second hers, and the third theirs! Look here," he was still staring at me in this disconcerting fashion, "you seem to know more about this dream than I do now. It isn't, by any chance, a book you've already thought out? I mean, that you're going to write one day?"

I determined to choke him off, once and for all. "Hardly my subject, I assure you!" and my voice held contempt.

"Oh, well . . ." he seemed abashed by my tone. "It was just an idea. You hear of funny things happening sometimes. Telepathy and all that. For a moment I wondered if I might have —well, tuned in to your mind, when I was asleep. Not that I've ever had any experience of that kind before, mind you."

"Nor I," and I turned once more to look out of the window at the flying dark, streaked by watery glimmers of light.

"Well, all I can say is," he declared fervently, "that I'd rather write that book than live it."

I decided to kill cleanly, and be done. Veiling the insolence of my reply in listlessness, I inquired. "Why, what happened?"

"But I've just told you! I've told you the most impressive bits. But it was the atmosphere of the book that was so awful, that somehow got you. A sort of suffocation; I can't describe it."

"Don't try. Take my advice and write it."

He smiled a little regretfully. "No," he said, "I know now I couldn't. But you can use the idea if you like."

(153

Suddenly the train ground over the points, we were approaching Victoria.

"It will make a fine story," he went on. "And it would be a funny thing if I ever came across it, once you had written it. But I don't like that title, if you don't mind my saying so. *Author Unknown.* Sounds like something out of the lonelyhearts column. I think you should try to get something a bit more artistic into the name. Something dreamy, if you know what I mean?"

"I will," I smiled grimly. "I will call it after you!"

"After me?"

"Yes." As the train ran into the station, I swung my bag from the rack. "I shall call it Joseph in immortal tribute to your powers of dream interpretation."

"Oh, I say!" he remonstrated, but by this time I had pushed my way into the corridor and escaped him.

The train was still moving when I jumped on to the platform. Already I was half an hour late. In the taxi I realized it would be well after midnight by the time I reached Grosvenor Crescent. A pity. At home no one expected me. My return, as so often happened, was unannounced. The front door would be bolted, and I would have to wait while Hammond unearthed himself from the basement. Fortunately I had dined well on the train.

As I mounted the steps to the silent house, I was somewhat surprised to see the drawing room lights aglow through the fog. And I noted that the curtains were only half drawn. Catherine should be in bed by this time. If she had stayed up reading, the natural thing would be to sit in her small study at the back of the house, where there was an electric fire, and only one lamp needed. Frankly I could not understand this unnecessary waste of electricity.

I tried my key in the lock, before ringing, and found it

open. This I confess startled me, as my rules are that unless we are entertaining, the front door is bolted at ten forty-five each night. In this way the staff are in bed by eleven, and early rising presents no problems.

I walked across to the dining room, and to my astonishment discovered my decanter and soda water were not in their proper place. A feeling of alarm replaced my surprise. What on earth could have happened?

Yet as I made my way upstairs, the house in other respects presented its normal appearance, luxurious, well tended. And this did something to reassure me. It will be realized by this time that although a writer by profession, I am no Bohemian. As a matter of fact, my hobby is antique furniture, and although my wife is much younger than I am, she happily shares my tastes.

I entered the brightly lit drawing room. It was empty. A large fire glowed on the hearth—absurdly large when I considered the lateness of the hour.

As I turned from this I caught sight of my decanter on its silver tray. It stood on a low table that usually holds a few choice books, and an engraved goblet with flowers.

It was almost as if I were expected.

But there were three glasses. Why three? Why two, for that matter?

I picked them up and examined them. They were clean.

As I replaced them, I moved the flowers in the Stuart goblet, my favorite Richmond roses, further from the heat, and in doing so noticed a valuable book of mine carelessly wedged in the William-and-Mary loveseat.

I picked it up. It was an expensively bound edition of Shakespeare's *Sonnets,* taken from my library downstairs, and my indignation was at once aroused, for already the pages gaped cruelly, as a bulky flower had been thrust among them to mark some passage or other. Not only was one page bruised, but a streak of damp discolored the opening lines of the sonnet opposite—the one beginning: "Let me not to the marriage of true minds admit impediments."

I hastily shook the flower onto the hearth, and, compressing the vellum covers of the book, replaced it on the table. I was looking round for a heavier volume to place on top of it, when I heard a step.

The next minute my wife came into the room.

"I thought it would be you," she said, and we kissed.

Almost at once I realized that she was laboring under some sort of agitation. Remembering the blazing lights, the wasteful fire, and my abused book, I could understand this.

She was dressed in a new velvet teagown that gave her slim figure an unusual look of opulence. The shade was a warm peach—too frivolous for the material I considered. My wife is a Titian beauty, and this peach shade formed rather a startling contrast with her copper-red hair and pearly skin. She looked seductive. But for the first time in my knowledge of her, less a lady than a woman.

"A new gown?" I inquired.

"Yes," she replied. "I took trouble with it." My wife has rather a disconcerting habit, at times, of anticipating an unspoken query in this way. I have never been certain if I like the trait or not. But she is a transparent creature.

"Doctor Richards has been here," she said. "He left about half an hour ago."

"Richards?"

"Yes," she sat down. "I suppose you've had something to eat?"

I ignored the question. "Why did he call at this hour? Most inconsiderate, surely?"

"I have not been well."

"What's been the matter? You look perfectly well. In fact you've got unusual color."

"It's my heart," she said, clasping and unclasping her hands rather nervously. "I told you about it before. But you seem to forget."

"I repeat," I said, "that I think it most inconsiderate of Richards to call at an hour like this."

"He's a busy man. He must come when he can," she replied in a listless way. "We must put up with it."

The resignation in her voice struck me as ridiculous under the circumstances. "On the contrary, we need not put up with it. When you complained about your health before, I told you to consult Sir Herbert Blakeney. Instead you continued with this overworked general practitioner, this nobody—"

"That's enough!" she interrupted me.

I stared at her. I could hardly believe my ears. But I continued, nevertheless, as if she had not spoken. "Instead you continue with this second-rate man. Well, let me tell you, I refuse to pay fees for advice I regard as worthless!"

"How dare you!" White with excitement, she leaped to her feet. It was the most unexpected attack of hysteria I have ever witnessed in anyone.

She stood there like a creature convulsed, as if she were choked by her own words.

"You snob," she cried, "you utter snob!"

My brain worked quickly. I knew I must deal with her condition at once. But I was at a disadvantage as I had never known her like this before.

"Sit down!" I commanded to gain time.

For a moment she hesitated, and then fell back into the chair.

"Control yourself," I continued, but hardly had the words left my lips than again she leaped to her feet. Brushing me aside, she fell on her knees by the hearth, and began groveling in the ashes.

"My flower," she cried brokenly, picking up the faded head, "my flower! And now it's burned . . . the hot ashes have burned it."

For a moment I forgot my annoyance with her. Her distress was quite moving. All trace of hysteria had left her. There was the same note of restraint in her voice as there had been in my traveling companion's when he spoke of the loss of his nearest and dearest—a suggestion of an authentic and limitless grief. Yet what difficulty a writer would have in reproducing this!

"I'm sorry," I said. "I did not know it was your flower. I found it disfiguring my book, and shook it on to the hearth."

"Book?" she said rather stupidly. Then her gaze traveled to the William-and-Mary loveseat. For the first time a look of guilt crossed her face.

"It doesn't matter," she said hurriedly. "I think I'll go to bed now, if you don't mind," and turned to the door.

"One moment!" I called. "You owe me some explanation. Why was that flower in my book?"

"I was trying to save it."

"Save it . . . why?"

"Doctor Richards brought it tonight. He had been to a funeral this afternoon . . . a pauper patient of his. It was all very sad. I had sent the poor woman a wreath. And he brought back one of the flowers from the grave."

"I'm sorry, Catherine. But you can perhaps understand my feelings when I found that bulky thing bruising my book."

"Yes," she said, "yes, of course . . . I think I'll go now. Goodnight."

Her fingers were on the handle of the door, when suddenly I remembered the dream of the man in the train.

"Stop a moment! What kind of wreath did you send her?"

She looked back, astonished. "White chrysanthemums . . . as you can see. The poor attach a lot of importance to flowers at funerals," she was staring at me almost defiantly.

"But why should Doctor Richards bring you this personal thing—a flower from her grave?"

"He thought I would like to have one."

"Did you ask him to bring you this . . . this souvenir?"

"No."

"It was entirely his own idea."

"What do you mean?" Suddenly she faced me, leaning back against the door, so that it shut. "What are you trying to force out of me?"

"The truth," I replied shortly, for by this time I had resolved to deal her a summary lesson. *"How long have you and this man been lovers?"*

"How dare you," she breathed, "how dare you suggest such an evil thing?"

"How dare he," I replied, "suggest such an evil thing to me? A doctor has greater license than other men. But let me remind you that like Caesar's wife, he must be above suspicion. You have heard no doubt, of a body known as the General Medical Council . . ."

"The General Medical Council," she repeated stupidly, "the General Medical Council!" Then her voice again rose on that unpleasant note of hysteria, "All these years I've borne with you, but there's still a way out. *And I shall take it!"*

"I'm afraid," I replied coldly, "that you will not get very far without money. Exactly what do you propose to do?"

But she could not sustain the dramatic note. Women

rarely can. They pitch a scene too high. And then peter out into the personal.

She gave me another sullen look. "That's my business!" she muttered, and on this anti-climax, left the room.

The scene had upset me, but less than might have been expected. I knew my wife well enough to realize that nothing of importance could have happened between them—although I would, of course, see that Richards' visits came to an end now.

No, at this point, the words of the man in the train had again gripped me.

I saw, all at once, that there was a story in his dream and my experience tonight. It would have to be deftly dealt with of course, but technical difficulties have always had a zest of their own for me.

I opened a drawer, and took out some paper.

Hastily I noted one or two points—for in this fictitious case, the wife would really betray her husband. Nevertheless, I would not make the discovery take place at midnight, on his unexpected return. No, that was too hackneyed. The flower might be found at any moment of any day. And as she stooped to retrieve it, the gift of her lover, the act would be virtually a theft. The husband watching her through the smoke of his cigarette, would remember his dream of her guilt! As the smoke cleared, they would confront each other in silence. He would say nothing. He could prove nothing. To all outward appearances, they would remain man and wife.

As I warmed to the idea, fatigue fell away from me. I began to write the opening paragraph, and then the story itself. My pen flew over the paper, but my thoughts flew faster. Often I stopped to jot down in advance a note, lest I forget it later. In an effortless rhythm I achieved my second wind.

Two o'clock struck, and three.

The traffic outside slackened, but never quite ceased. I worked on oblivious of all but intermittent sound. At two o'clock I had been startled for a moment by a loud report in the silence, the tire of some motor car, no doubt. And I had raised my head to listen. The sound might have come from under my own roof. But as the traffic thinned outside, the room grew still, and my work continued apace.

At the end of two hours I arose, tingling in mind and body; restored by the well-being that work under such conditions invariably generates; conscious of that odd purification that always follows when the arrow sings to its mark.

Suddenly I realized I was hungry.

I crossed the floor and rang the bell.

All at once I remembered the hour, and that everyone was in bed. The place was quite quiet.

Everyone must be asleep. I could expect nothing hot. There was nothing else for it . . . I must put up with cold fare.

As I turned off the drawing-room light, I listened once more, in the darkness.

Yes, to take refuge in a cliché, the house was as silent as the dead.

The Lady of
Great Occasions

A Story
for Children

The Lady of Great Occasions

This elderly lady I write about was a charlady called Mrs. Brushett, who lived off the Euston Road, just within shrieking distance of the Great Northern Express. Far up above the smoke and the roar and the traffic of the station she lived in one of those strangely dead, drab streets beside it, in a three-room bandbox with Mrs. Annie Abbot, and Edgar Alf, aged eight.

Now both Mrs. Brushett and Mrs. Annie Abbot were widows (Mrs. Brushett sadly, and Mrs. Annie Abbot gladly) and Edgar Alf aged eight was the apple of both their eyes, though they showed their love in different ways. Mrs. Annie Abbot slapped him daily, gave him physic weekly, and scoldings before and after every naughty thing he did; while Mrs. Brushett soothed and kissed him and gave him an orange stealthily each time he'd been punished for being a bad, ungrateful boy. Between them

(165

both Edgar Alf grew up with rather dazed ideas as to what was really expected of him.

Yet, he accepted them both philosophically enough, just as he accepted their cupboard home above the station, the steam, the smuts, the whistles, and the unending throb of hurrying things below. Like the engines they were in his blood. He could not have imagined life upon the Earth World without them.

Now, on the day this story starts just as the one-thirty shrieked itself out of the cavern below her, Mrs. Brushett lay back in bed with a sigh of absolute contentment. One month ago, exactly to the day, she had broken her leg. Never in all her days had she known such a time, such peace, such rest—and the kind people who had run her over paying for everything, and even sending her flowers! Her, Bella Brushett! And a card each time with "Compliments" on it. Mrs. Brushett didn't know which meant most to her.

The cards, three in number, were arranged upon the mantel shelf, the flowers in a jug by her bed.

Lying back she smiled widely all over her vague-looking face. "Quite the Quality!" she told herself, almost with a giggle at the idea.

At the sound of a footstep outside, she tried hurriedly to smooth some of the smile off her face, for it was a Thursday, and Thursday was Mrs. Abbot's day to "do" the Mothers' Meeting at the Town Hall—and the thing that ruffled Mrs. Abbot most was serving tea professionally to those who were, she knew, no better than herself.

"Well, there you are," she observed gloomily, entering as if there were three of her. "Now, don't you go getting too uplifted over those there cards, or something will happen. It allus does. Remember wot happened to Minnie Parker after her brother got that printed invite to that Masonic dinner. *She* started collecting them, and after she got four different kinds, and was burstin' with glory, her Emma went off in a galloping consumption."

"Ma!" from the front room shouted Edgar Alf, who was being kept indoors on the strength of a purely imaginary sore throat. "Ma! Quick! The messenger's coming down the street again with a bunch of red flowers the size of a roll of linoleum!"

"Wot!" cried Mrs. Abbot, turning crimson. "H'another?"

"Heavings," murmured Mrs. Brushett lying back weak with excitement.

"Now, then, Alf!" threatened his mother, "don't you dare go to the door with that face on you. Just wait till I've changed my apron. And see who's looking out. Quick, now!"

"Mrs. Murphy an' Mrs. Skinner's both looking out," Edgar Alf reported loudly.

"Quiet now!" Mrs. Abbot admonished him.

"And Mrs. Murphy called over to Miss Tibett, an' she's looking out now, too," buzzed Edgar Alf in a husky whisper.

"Go on," commended his mother, breathlessly tying her apron around her. "Is Mrs. Parker watching too?"

"No-o-o!" called Alf, "she ain't."

"If that ain't like her!" said Mrs. Abbot crossly, "and if it was bailiffs she'd be there on the front step with h'opera glasses."

"Well! I'm all of a-tremble," confessed Mrs. Brushett weakly. "If this ain't an Occasion I don't know wot is!"

"Now, you keep cool, Bella Brushett," warned Mrs. Abbot, "or you'll be having a stroke you will."

"Ma!" shouted Edgar Alf again. "He's turned into the close, and Mrs. Parker is a-following of him up."

"Well, if that ain't Providence!" exclaimed Mrs. Brushett thankfully.

"Now then," hissed Mrs. Abbot, "you lie back, and don't

be too free with how you're feeling. I'll ope the door to her with the flowers, and you mark my words—every one of her relations'll have been laid to rest in wreaths of them!"

Two minutes later the bare little bedroom with the treacherous three-legged chair, and the obstinate chest of drawers that never opened without a struggle, and would only shut with a bang, was full of flowers, flowers such as Mrs. Brushett had never seen before. Riotously, extravagantly, they glowed now in her own meager room, before her startled and delighted eyes—great spikes of rosy tubelike lilies, speckled as orchids, their velvety parted lips stained with black pollen, and breathing a perfume heady as incense. Behind this mass of color and scent the faces of Minnie Parker and Annie Abbot hovered like unreal brown paper masks, things that looked to Mrs. Brushett for the first time like a mistake somehow.

"Well, Mrs. B., you 'ave got a show and no mistake," said Mrs. Parker, insinuating herself at once into the one and only three-legged chair. "I was always partial to a lily myself. My wedding bookay had five of those done up in it with a taste of maidenhair, and though I says it myself, it were the smartest I ever seen."

"Wot are they called?" said Mrs. Brushett, "H'arums?"

"H'arums!" scoffed Mrs. Abbot, "you're forgetting your Bible already. "H'arums is white, standing stiff up like pokers—only doing nothin' as Solomon said. Now these," her head on one side, she paused for a minute, "these is running all over the place like a kind of pink Madonna."

"Pink Madonna," nodded Mrs. Parker firmly, "that's wot they are. I remember arsking for that distinctly, I was always a one for somethin' h'outstanding."

"Well," said Mrs. Abbot, "don't go exciting the h'invalid. I'm off now. I'm on the tray this afternoon."

"Well, you soon won't be," called Mrs. Parker impressively over her shoulder, "for the Mothers is going on strike next week against coming to the Thursday treats again."

"Wotever for?" asked Mrs. Brushett, startled, shocked, and deeply interested.

"Well, would you believe it," Mrs. Parker leaned forward confidentially, "but because the Committee never got more nor half their teaspoons back, last time the Mothers got four inches of macaroni to stir their tea with." She leaned back triumphantly.

"It do seem a bit pointed," agreed Mrs. Brushett.

"Well, wot I want to know," said Mrs. Parker rearing again proudly before them both, "is if the Church can't afford to lose a few teaspoons, 'oo can? And as Mrs. Gallacher said to me, is this the Christian way to turn the other cheek?"

"Saves washing," said Mrs. Abbot argumentatively.

"Low-down suspicion," said Mrs. Parker, darkly.

"Annie," said Mrs. Brushett firmly, "I think I'd like to get some sleep." Oh! why couldn't they go and leave her alone with her wonderful flowers, alone, in peace to drink them into her very heart so that she would never forget them long after they were withered.

At last they were moving towards the door, then Mrs. Parker exclaimed in horror. "You don't mean to say, Annie, that you're a-going to leave a delicate woman like that with an open window and you not back till six tonight and all the evening air off the street getting in at her?"

"Doctor's orders," announced Mrs. Abbot.

"Doctors!" cried Mrs. Parker in such an outraged voice that both the others stared at her. "Doctors! Don't speak of doctors to me! It was the doctor in Clapham that killed my Emily. Yes, made her lie in a through draft day *and* night, till she caught her death, did Emily. And when I says to Pa, I says, 'Pa, he's killing Emily!' Pa says to me, he says, 'Oh, come now, Ma, don't take

on so. After all the man's had a kind o' training, stands to reason
he must know more'n you or me. 'Sides, we're payin him.' So I
give in, and Emily died." And Mrs. Parker broke into undoubted
sobs.

"Annie," said Mrs. Brushett, a little alarmed, "shut the
window, there's a dear, do . . . and tell Alf to ope it before he
lets the doctor in."

"Orlright," said Mrs. Abbot, slamming down the window.
"But you're weak—as I have allus held, Bella."

A minute later Mrs. Brushett was alone, alone with that
great glow of color. She leaned forward, and touched one of the
stamens with her water withered fingers. It left a velvet smear
across them. Mrs. Brushett was fascinated.

A little movement made her turn her head. Edgar Alf
had wriggled in on his stomach with the bread lid on his back,
and a clothespin on his nose, and a sound of troubled breathing.
She knew at once he was being a snail for her amusement.

"Oh, Alf!" she said weakly, "you know you didn't ought!"
Slowly the snail climbed on to her bed, and then she noticed that
its mouth was fearsomely distended.

"Edgar Alf!" she cried, "put that out at once, you bad,
ungrateful boy. If you swallow that, you'll have an appendix, you
will. As if we 'adn't 'ad enough trouble without you temp'ing
Providence."

Slowly the snail disgorged a small, dark gleaming object,
which fell on the faded counterpane.

"Why! Wotever is it?" said Mrs. Brushett, picking it up
curiously.

"It's a present," said Edgar Alf, "from me."

"But what a heathenish looking thing!" exclaimed Mrs.
Brushett, examining it more closely. "Wherever did you get it?"

"I found it," said Edgar Alf, loudly and emphatically.

"Now, then!" she answered warningly.

"I found it," he repeated, "true's I breave. Underneaf old Isaac's table, the one standing with its front legs in the street."

Mrs. Brushett sighed feebly. She knew that was as near the truth as she or any one would ever get.

"And if you don't like it," he announced indignantly, "I'll take it back. I can swop it for two golf balls or a razor any day."

"No, no, dearie," said Mrs. Brushett quickly. "It's—" She could not quite manage the word pretty. "It's not every one, I'm sure, as has such a queer lookin' thing. Now, run away, there's a love, do, and let me get a wink of sleep."

"Hoot-toot-toot!" shrilled Edgar Alf, fearsomely, and she knew him instantly in his triumph for the two-thirty departing platform nine. With a rattle he slammed the bread lid on his head, uttering a piercing whistle and swung out on the open door. And again she knew him as that last-minute wonder, the guard of every train. "Klick-klack!" she responded mechanically, for was she not the signal box?—and the two-thirty well away.

And now that she was quite alone, Mrs. Brushett's head felt strangely dreamy, and yet not heavy. She did not feel that she could sleep, and yet she longed to close her eyes. She determined that she would in one, two minutes, but first of all she must take one other look at her forest of rosy lilies. What curious tangled shadows their fresh green leaves flung upon the plain distemper of the wall. Gray shadows, shifting shadows, lifting shadows. Of what did they remind her? Ah! now she knew. The hurt place in her mind where she never dared to linger since the day that Terry died. And now for the first time in many years she found herself remembering it without any feeling of pain—just a kind of wistfulness, green shadows, shifting shadows, lifting shadows under the great chestnut trees in Greenwich Park.

That was where, when Mrs. Brushett had been twenty-five, and imagined no one would ever love her now, that Terry had proposed to her. That proposal was the most treasured memory in her recollection, because Mrs. Brushett felt quite sure no one, in her position, had ever had a proposal like it.

Under a great chestnut tree (how clearly she saw it still) they had sat close together one bland evening, and Terry, pointing to the tall, stiff flowers among the branches, had exclaimed, "How's that for candles free of charge?" (What a one he had been for thinking thoughts no one else ever had!) And she remembered how next he'd run his hand across the strange, regular tracery on the great rough bark, so deeply rutted there that it seemed as if carved on purpose—and had asked her, "Now what will that be putting you in mind of, with me sitting close beside you?"

"I dunno," she had replied stupidly. "Just wood."

"Ijut!" he had said lovingly "it's like churches—for all the world like churches round about the painted windows." Then he'd drawn a little closer, his head so near her shoulder that her heart had thumped like a door knocker at midnight when somebody sounds it suddenly—and very confidentially he'd added, "Now it will be being night time in our church, with candles lit above—and you and me inside the church, a-standing by the altar! And the spook that lives in the chestnut tree is a-saying to you and me, 'Terence O'Malley Brushett, will you be for taking this woman to be your wedded wife?' "

"Oh! Terry!" she cried, half laughing, half shocked, "You are a one—but you didn't ought."

"And I says 'I will,' " Terry continued. "But the spook what lives in the chestnut tree says, 'That's not enough,' says he, 'the p'int is, will she have you?' And that's what I want to be knowin', as soon as you find it convenient."

No, truly, as Mrs. Brushett looked back, no one she felt

certain, outside the gentry, had ever had such a fancy proposal. Indeed so fancy had it been that for some time after she had sometimes wondered if it were really real.

And then a year after they were married, Terry (who was a painter by trade) had fallen from a top-story window, and smashed himself like an eggshell on the pavement beneath. Mrs. Brushett remembered how Annie had cried and wept for a whole week. Annie was Terry's stepsister. But Mrs. Brushett had never wept at all. That was what had seemed so strange at the time. Mrs. Brushett knew now it was because it hadn't seemed real to her—Terry who was the *realist* thing in life to be smashed like an eggshell. No, it wasn't real! It couldn't be. Terry, she knew, must be alive somewhere, *somehow*—only she couldn't get at him.

That is how Mrs. Brushett felt about the saddest thing that ever happened to her (how she felt about the saddest thing that overtook each of those around her in a different way). It might be *true*, as she knew it had happened, but it wasn't real, for all that. That is what she felt although she could not have explained if she had tried. And although a pale, mild body, and one you'd never notice on a brilliant red-letter day, this shining belief of hers made her a kind of beamy lantern to those around her, on that black day we all find marked within our calendar sometime —that day of sorrowful occasion. And many there were who lit their snuffed-out hopes from her mild and constant ardor, though not all remembered her when daylight broke as usual later on.

All this I must explain to you, else you would not understand all the beauty and the wonder of the thing that now befell her, for as she lay there in her poor, neat room gazing at the rose-colored lilies pouring their beauty from the old cracked jug, it suddenly struck her that their shadow was behaving with far more animation than was usual to any flowers knee-deep in water and repose. It seemed to shake and shiver on the wall. The more she stared the more it seemed to shower itself over the drab distemper. She sat upright in bed to make quite sure she was not dreaming. No! There it was in movement still—as if keeping time now to her own tumultuous breathing.

Mrs. Brushett lay back with a gasp. "Well," she confessed aloud, "if I'm a-moving these from here with nothing more nor breaving, I'm a lors to the 'All of Mysteries, I am."

As she spoke the room darkened, not in any threatening way, but in mellow fashion—gently the shadow of the lilies spread completely over the walls, then completely over the roof, dappling the room in a leafy way, until even the shabby patched bed quilt seemed to tremble with dark little islands of shade afloat in a sea of light. "Now, then," Mrs. Brushett remonstrated anxiously with herself, "if the wall paper 'ad 'ad a pattern, I would 'ave said I was the victim of a h'optical delusion—but it ain't . . . I must be going barmy," she added in distress.

Thicker and thicker the leaf shadows fell, faster and faster they whirled upon Mrs. Brushett. Gray shadows, falling shadows turned to green shadows, lifting shadows, and the very air seemed on a sudden painted with a light, a brilliance that dazzled her. She was next aware of a hundred little rustling noises she had not heard before, then of water purling from some damp, green place, of a hundred little airs fresh with country grasses, woods and flowers playing upon her tired, town face. Mrs. Brushett had the topsy-turvy feeling that she was being lulled—not to sleep, but awake. Softly she shut her eyes.

Then as she lay there very still, eyes shut, but more aware than she had ever been, she suddenly knew that she lay no longer under the patched bed quilt, but under a great chestnut tree shedding its leaves in a summer gale. No sooner had she realized this than she heard a deep voice say, "Time to wake up."

Opening her eyes with an effort, she saw before her a tall figure, hidden in shining armor—and behind him a great sweep of wind-swept sky. From beneath his feet the short cropped downs rolled steeply away, then flowed gradually into the low-lying heavens, whose far horizon lay soaked in a sun-haze that blurred the dark blobs of the farthest trees in an aureole of gold.

Mrs. Brushett, with feelings of the liveliest astonishment, discovered she was lying on the outskirts of a dense wood, that in front of her lay this open prospect, soaked in sunshine and the smell of myrtle and wild thyme; while immediately before her stood this commanding figure in shining armor.

"Time to wake up," he repeated gently.

"Well, I never!" exclaimed Mrs. Brushett, a trifle flustered. "You 'ave given me a bit of a start coming up so sudden-like."

"Don't you remember me?" asked the tall Knight in a surprised, inquiring tone of voice.

Mrs. Brushett peered at him closely with her vague blue eyes. "Well, just for the moment," she said politely, "I don't think as I do." Then her face cleared swiftly. "Well, now, if that wasn't silly of me!" she exclaimed. "Of course you're the gentleman out of the Knight's Castile Soap advertisement. Why! I don't know how often I 'aven't cut you out for Edgar Alf of a Saturday evening when he 'adn't anythink better to do."

The tall Knight of Castile saluted in a fashionable kind of way, removed his gauntlet with ceremony, and held out a large, fine hand. Mrs. Brushett shook it nervously. "Pleased to meet you, I'm sure," she faltered.

The Knight of Castile patted her hearteningly on the shoulder. "Prepare," he said royally, "to enjoy yourself as you never have before. Prepare for Joy with a capital J. This is Your Great Day Off!"

"Did ever!" exclaimed Mrs. Brushett, politely, secretly very much dazed. "I'm sure," she added, "I'm very much obliged to you. And if you could tell me whereabouts I've got to . . ."

The tall Knight took her hand, and sweeping his arm towards the somber wood, so murmurous with creaking boughs and rustling secrets, so chill with scents of damp and earth and leaves—he answered her. "Your Day Off has now arrived. You are standing at last in the Valley of the Shadow."

Mrs. Brushett turned pale with anxiety, and sat down heavily on a fallen-tree stump.

"You don't mean to tell me," she said in a deeply shocked voice, "that I'm dead and never knew it?"

"Believe me," said the tall Knight cordially, "you have never been more alive, but the life you lived off Euston Station is now a thing of the past. This is truly the Valley of the Shadow, as you Earth People guess it to be, but it is the Valley of the Shadow of Heaven—a thing they forget to add." And he led her out of the wood towards the sunny downland rolling to the windy sky.

"Well, I'm sure," said Mrs. Brushett, mopping her face a little feverishly, "you mean well, but I'm taken all of a heap, I am."

"There is nothing to be alarmed about," said the Knight of Castile very graciously in that serene, mellow voice of his (where had she heard those tones before—somewhere quite recently, surely?). "When each mortal comes to the close of their work on Earth, they are granted their big Day Off, before they pass on to the country of Tomorrow which you on Earth call Heaven. Here in the valley between they may spend their day as on Earth they have earned it."

"You don't tell me," said Mrs. Brushett in a horrified voice, stopping dead as she spoke, "you don't tell me that I've got into Purgatory—and me Church of England and my mother before me?"

"Come, come," said the tall Knight soothingly, "there is nothing here to distress you. Why worry yourself with words? What's in a name, at any rate?"

"That's from the Bible, anyway," said Mrs. Brushett, relieved, her face smoothing itself out a little, "but where are we going to now?" For by this time she felt rather tired, the wood lay some distance behind them, and they were walking together rapidly over those sun swept downs which led apparently into the sky, and nowhere else, as far as Mrs. Brushett could see.

"Do you see that Well?" questioned the Knight, pointing to a low stone circle before them, which she had not noticed before. "Well, when we reach it, you will drink of its waters, and be fit to enjoy your Day Off."

"Did ever!" exclaimed Mrs. Brushett appreciatively. "Well, I'm sure that will be a treat, for I've never yet got the good out of a Bank Holiday jaunt what with washing up extra the night before to be ready. I only hope," she added, as they approached the Well, "that it's safe, as I've never been one to drink strange water in the open."

"But this is bottled," explained the Knight, gracefully lifting from the stone circle a tray on which stood a large brown bottle and a very spindle-legged wine glass. From a fruit-wreathed label round the bottle's neck, the Knight read in clear and definite tones, tones with no nonsense about them:

> "Build Up Her Strength
> Do It Today
> Tomorrow May Be Too LATE."

(Again Mrs. Brushett wondered where had she seen those hands before, the palms so strong, the fingers so nimble?)

"Now, shut your eyes, and snap it up," he commanded, "for your Day Off is about to begin," and she had the feeling that he was smiling gently behind his silver vizor.

A little nervously she shut her eyes and swallowed.

Then she opened them, and lo! she was standing in a handsome street full of tall, bright buildings, with dark roofs that gleamed with a sparkle of rain, and a paveway that lay cool, freshly moistened below, though above the sky shone a magical blue as if it had been enameled—as good every bit as the Lake Como poster that splashed Euston grayness with color.

"Good 'Eavings," said Mrs. Brushett, breathlessly, "but what 'ave you done to the country side?"

"This was all here before," said the tall Knight in an explanatory way, "only you were too tired to see it. You only saw then as much as you could stand. It is all we ever do."

"Well, you *are* a one," said Mrs. Brushett, admiringly. "Regular quick change h'artist you are. 'Ere today and gorn tomorrow."

"That unfortunately is my motto," said the tall Knight regretfully, raising a mournful hand, "but pray don't remind me yet of the hour when we must part."

But Mrs. Brushett did not hear him. Eagerly she was scanning the gay little shops on either side, where some behind tiny bright windows were full of things to eat—all laid out so temptingly like the American food in *The Ladies' Home Journal*—and where others were full of things to wear from the extremist type of Parisian vogue, down to glass earrings from Venice, and the finest Wolsey Wear. Up and down the paveway, people passed in a happy, leisurely way, shopping with gay baskets on their arms, and chubby children, like Virol beauties, running at their heels.

Mrs. Brushett gasped with pleasure, then remembering

her soiled and shabby clothes she shrank against the shop window nearest.

"What does your mirror tell you?" quoted the tall Knight, patting her helpfully on the shoulder. Mrs. Brushett lifted a tearful gaze to the window, and as she did so, her eyes widened with astonishment. There in the reflection before her she saw the Knight of Castile standing gallantly beside a modish-looking figure clad in the very squirrel cape she had so often admired in Saunder's window (off the Euston Road) and bearing airily a patent leather reticule (with handsomely embossed monogram) and a military umbrella, and finally topped by a toque of unbelievable smartness which radiated a shower of ospreys at a dangerously acute angle.

Mrs. Brushett felt her head reel. "Well, how's that?" queried the tall Knight in his heartening way.

Mrs. Brushett blushed. "I always favored gray," she admitted, "but I never thought to see the day I'd carry squirrel."

"We'll go in here," said the tall Knight then, opening a shop door, under a swinging sign marked X.Y.Z., "and have a bite of something. Now, just name your fancy," he added hospitably, as they sat down at a tiny table laid for two.

Mrs. Brushett blushed again. "Well," she said, apologetically, "as you're so kind, I always was a one for a bit of fried fish —and perhaps a drop of beer."

"One fried fish, one steak and onions, and one large Guinness," ordered the Knight of Castile in a reckless, good-as-you kind of way of the trimmest, frilliest waitress Mrs. Brushett had ever seen. This, Mrs. Brushett realized, was Life at last.

The next minute their meal, served on paper plates, was set before them. "If that ain't the slickest ever," exclaimed Mrs. Brushett, "and never no washing up needed after, neither."

"Afterwards," said the Knight of Castile, pouring out a

frothing glass, "we shall drive or walk round the town and then visit the Grand Bohemian Cinema de Luxe. Whichever you prefer."

"Well," said Mrs. Brushett more confidentially after half a pint of stout had vanished, "if it's all the same to you, I'd like to see as much sitting as possible. You haven't a notion wot a treat it is to have the day to sit down in." Then leaning a little nearer him so that the pleasant people, eating so contentedly at the surrounding tables, could not hear her, she whispered a little nervously, "This isn't Paris, is it? I can't see no names nowhere."

"This town is your own capital, dear lady," replied the tall Knight in the way that had appealed to Mrs. Brushett from the beginning as being distinctly French.

"That it ain't," she answered with firmness. "Where's the noise and rush, the motor buses and the dirty buildings, and the smell of petrol in your very food."

"Ah!" said the Knight, smiling behind his half-raised vizor, "I must explain. This town with all its handsome buildings, spacious streets, and wealthy shops belongs to one person (who created it out of nothing you might say) and to whom these people round about us are most devoted subjects—the Lady of Great Occasions."

"Just fancy that!" said Mrs. Brushett admiringly. "If that don't beat the band."

"Indeed," continued the tall Knight helping himself liberally to meringue, "she is one of the richest women, not through inheritance you understand, as we don't believe in that kind of short cut here, but through her own direct effort. Believe me, I am proud to be sitting opposite her." And he bowed again in his stylish way.

Mrs. Brushett turned peony-crimson, and then went lily-white. "You're having me on!" she whispered shamefaced, "and I don't take it kindly in you."

"Let me assure you," said the tall Knight earnestly, "I am far from having you on—I am only having you out, for this town is your very own. Its buildings rise from your own brave hopes, its clean, bright streets are peopled with your own loving thoughts; its riches are gathered from the fullness of all your hard-worked days, from the wealth of your kindly deeds—for on Earth you were very truly a Lady of Sorrowful Occasions. See now, as we leave this shop, how your subjects bow to you gratefully."

Pink with confusion, and more conscious of her feet and hands than she had ever been, Mrs. Brushett followed the tall Knight from the shop. Once in the open she clutched his arm. "It's too much," she said, "that's wot it is. Too much. I was always one for a back seat. Now if Annie Abbot was 'ere, she could carry it h'off with a 'igh 'and, but I'm taken all of a 'eap, I am, and I'll only give you a red face, I will."

The Knight took out a whistle, and blew a shrill blast. Instantly round the marble corner of the street, under the blue-enameled sky, reflecting its color in a radiant silver surface, there swept the largest, emptiest charabanc Mrs. Brushett had ever seen.

"In you pop," said the Knight, and into the two best seats they climbed. "Drive through the town for an hour or so—and then to the Grand Bohemian Cinema de Luxe," ordered the Knight, and for over an hour down those broad, clean streets they swept, with bowing smiling faces on either hand, among the tall white buildings with dark, sparking roofs above, and glossy, leafy trees below until at last they drew up at a vast glass building, more like the Crystal Palace than anything Mrs. Brushett had ever seen, with a great flight of milk white stairs bounding up to it.

"The Grand Bohemian Cinema de Luxe," announced the Knight royally.

"*Well!*" said Mrs. Brushett, alighting and drawing her longest breath of wonder yet, "if this don't knock Alexandra Palace silly I don't know what do." Then her face dimmed, and a tired look came into her eyes. "Those steps will take a bit of doing," she reflected aloud. "I only 'ope they put two chars on the job."

"Behold!" answered the tall Knight pressing a brass knob on the marble stairway, "your washing day a thing of leisure! Done while you wait! Likewise, no more stiff backs and tired arms!" And as he spoke, from the top step a fairy fountain issued, spraying the steps with a crystal shower.

"Well, if that ain't an extenshun of the limit," said Mrs. Brushett, glistening with admiration and moisture—then, as swiftly, her face changed, "but wot about the chars?" she asked, "there ain't no work for them, that's plain, so how can they get a living?"

"Some of them," said the Knight as he led her up the steps to the box office, "are writing poetry, and some of them are painting pictures, and all of them are spending money most extravagantly. In short, they are now enjoying to the full all those very things they lacked on earth before their Day Off dawned.

"Which seats?" demanded the hidden personage behind the office grill in the intimidating, coldly superior way that such hidden personages have.

"The best," replied the Knight without a moment's hesitation, slapping down two half crowns on the spot. Again Mrs. Brushett had a sensation of giddiness. As they entered the friendly darkness of the theatre, she caught the Knight's arm.

"Oh! if only Edgar Alf was here," she whispered, "it seems too bad me having all this by my lonesome." The tall

Knight pressed her elbow sympathetically, but replied, "I told you this was *your* Day Off. Edgar Alf has not yet earned his, and when he does he will want to spend it in a very different way."

"He's such a one for trains and noise!" said Mrs. Brushett, apologetically, "but 'ow did you know that?"

"Wait and see," said the Knight, and again there seemed to Mrs. Brushett something familiar in his words as well as in his voice.

"Programme?" inquired an attendant with refinement from the darkness.

"Naturally," said the Knight in a pained tone of voice, and as they sat down in the very best seats, the theatre blossomed into light, revealing a hundred golden pillars, and a thousand swinging baskets of richly perfumed flowers, all elegantly tied up on one side with broad bows of satin ribbon. The next minute the word "Interval" flashed weakly on the screen. "Well, if that ain't lucky," said Mrs. Brushett in tones of congratulation, "now we know we've missed nothing, for say wot you like, it's never the same coming in at the end of the drama, and working your way back to the beginning, with the comic turns sandwiched between."

"My sentiments to a T," said the tall Knight heartily. *"Which* reminds me!" and turning his head he called in his stylish way, "tea for two!" and slapped down two shillings before him.

Again Mrs. Brushett had a sensation of giddiness. "You know, you didn't ought," she breathed, "spending your money like water on me."

"Mine is the pleasure," replied the Knight with such a gallant bow it quite went to Mrs. Brushett's head. Blushingly she slipped her finger under the sixpenny tag on the programme—the first she had ever opened. Inside she read:

(183

Rathé's Daily Budget
"TO KNOW MUCH IS TO SEE MUCH"
followed by
"THE COMEDY OF MINNIE PARKER"
and
"THE LIFE OF EDGAR ALF"

"Heavings," gasped Mrs. Brushett, "you don't mean to say as how we're going to watch *them* really?" Breathing deeply she turned to Part Two of the programme—but the tall Knight hid the lettering with his hand. *"That* belongs to a later date," he remarked, "meantime snap up this tea."

Gratefully Mrs. Brushett gulped it down, her eyes still round with wonder. "Well, if this ain't an Occasion!" she murmured. "Why! I wouldn't call the king my cousin."

As she spoke the theatre darkened, and the screen bloomed forth in color, and lo! Mrs. Brushett was watching ladies (not a bit younger than herself, and not a bit better looking) trying on squirrel coats and skunk collars against a background of prize chrysanthemums, and then donning hats, some of them not half so smart as her present one, before mounting cars (quite half the size of her silver charabanc)—to motor to bazaars or launches on the Clyde or similar scenes of pleasure.

The screen darkened for a moment, and then glowed again, this time with the name of "Minnie Parker."

Mrs. Brushett settled herself back in her chair, in an enjoyable way, and lo! the next minute there was Minnie Parker as a baby in her cradle, before her admiring parents, clutching at the flowers in the district visitor's hat; Mrs. Parker in her christening shawl snatching feverishly at air; Mrs. Parker at the age of three—to her parents' amusement, grasping handfuls of hair from anyone who had the misfortune to approach her; Mrs.

Parker at the age of four, a plump infant with a still plumper underlip, grabbing for good the teddy bear belonging to her little cousin—to the music of her parents' exclamation, "Well! what a little one you are."

In the darkness Mrs. Brushett felt her cheeks growing a little warm. This was rather how she felt she sometimes treated Edgar Alf. Mrs. Parker flashed again upon the screen, Mrs. Parker at every size, at every moment, in every attitude. Mrs. Parker at the age of eight, of twelve, of sixteen, and twenty. Always striving to go one better than the person next her, and always managing somehow—anyhow. History repeating itself repeatedly—Mrs. Parker at the age of twenty-four capturing the sweetheart of her little cousin much as she had captured her teddy bear once upon a time—not so much because she wanted either as because she couldn't bear to be without that which someone else possessed.

"I can't think why this is called a comic, I can't," whispered Mrs. Brushett to the Knight. "I call it 'eart breaking, I do."

The tall Knight shook his head. "Only for the lookers on," he answered. "She's quite satisfied, because each time she gets what she wants, you see. And when she finds it isn't what she thought, she just grabs something else. Her mind is like a curiosity shop full of other people's treasures. She can't make use of them because she doesn't understand them, and she daren't sell them because she could only do this at a loss now. Her life has become a lumber room full of unwanted bits." Mrs. Parker at the age of thirty now appeared upon the screen. "You see," said the tall Knight, "she is worn out already gathering those bits and pieces that she covets, but has no real use for. Now she begins in thought, and word and deed, to take from those around her— and every day she does this she becomes more unreal, more of a nightmare to herself and others. See, there she is at forty—and now we have her as she is at present, fifty-two at Whitsun, with a glimmering of the truth, aching to be herself at last."

"Poor soul," said Mrs. Brushett, "I never was wot you'd call partial to her, but seeing her all spread out before me, I can't help feeling as 'ow her parents ought to have been different, and not spoiled her. Yet I carn't help feeling sorry for them, too, as it would all begin so gradual."

"My sentiments to a T," said the Knight again. "In your Earth World, they believed to see much was to know much, but we believe quite differently here. We feel that to know much is to see much, and so we think twice before we spoil our own, at the cost of other people's, and in thinking twice, our own think once at least."

"Well," said Mrs. Brushett, "she's earned her day off if any one ever has. Thin as a potato peeling she is now, poor thing, and always on the jump."

"Her Day Off will also be very different from yours," said the Knight in a thoughtful voice. "Yes, very different. She will spend its entire twelve hours in being her real self at last—and nothing else will she do. That will be her day of rest before she passes into the Country of Tomorrow."

" 'Eaven?" said Mrs. Brushett a little nervously. Then she added timidly in a whisper, "If it isn't too much of a liberty, would you mind giving me a notion of what it's really like? You hear so many different things, and all of them sounding strange like. I like the notion of the Pearly Gates, but the golden streets," her voice became apologetic, "always seem to me so hard to the feet for heaven."

"Each of us sees it differently on arrival," said the tall Knight slowly, "each of us sees it according to the light that's in us. Some of these lights are flaming beacons flaring wildly, some are torches burning splendidly, some are tranquil lamps shining serenely, some are pale as candlelight at early dawn—but it doesn't matter how great or small your light is (that is the wonderful thing about heaven) the Country of Tomorrow is the land where at last each one of us can put our best foot forward unhampered by ourselves."

"By ourselves?" repeated Mrs. Brushett in a dim voice.

"Yes, didn't you know?" said the Knight. "Life in the old Earth World is always an obstacle race to be sure, and the worst hurdle is nearly always our very own selves. And that obstacle is always the last we tackle. If we tackled it first," he sighed, "nothing else would ever seem hard."

"Well, I never," said Mrs. Brushett, "you do have a way of saying things mixed, and then putting them plain. If I'd only thought like that I might 'ave bin a better woman."

"No," said the tall Knight gravely, "from the beginning you have been the Lady of Sorrowful Occasions—from the beginning your obstacle has been an infinitely more tragic one, an infinitely harder one to overcome—for yours has never been yourself, but always someone you loved."

"D'you mind," said Mrs. Brushett in a dazed way, "saying that again differently."

"Well," answered the tall Knight quietly, "your danger lies not in loving yourself, but another—not in loving that other too much, but not loving that other wisely enough. You have always loved with both eyes shut. Blind man's buff, and kiss-in-the-ring, those are the games you have played invisibly with Edgar Alf. Never once did you teach him follow the leader, though in your mind you must have known, sooner or later out in the world he was bound to go through the mill."

Mrs. Brushett hung her head, and in a shamefaced way she answered, "I know I haven't bin as firm as I ought sometimes with him, but he's the lovingest little fellow—I never knowed his equal for getting colds in the chest in July. And Annie, for all she loves him dearly, is always a-scolding at him and an upsetting of him."

"Well, well!" said the tall Knight from the darkness, and the tone of his voice seemed to resolve all conflict in understanding. "Look at this now!" and the screen suddenly glowed with these potent words:

"THE LIFE OF EDGAR ALF"

Mrs. Brushett's hand went to her heart. She leaned forward in her chair. Edgar Alf in print before her! Her Edgar Alf! Always she had known he was different from ordinary children. Why the very way he'd teethed had been different; everything had always been more difficult with him than anyone else. Her Edgar Alf!

The screen flashed, and there he was on the big pillow in the old double bed in the kitchen—not one of your great, bouncing fat babies, but such a lively little follow with his pale skin, and dark ringed eyes, and that tiny, smooth moist mouth of his. And his little naked feet! No baby ever had such clever, moving feet. For all the world like a pair of hands they were, so active. And his fingers, his tiny clinging fingers with the baby nails so sharp, so perfect! Once more her heart seemed to wound her with longing, as she gazed again at the ridiculous looking tuft of honey-colored hair that stuck up above his ears, and the necklace of faint warm creases in his tiny, helpless neck.

Again the screen flashed, and there was Edgar Alf, aged two, with his first cold in the chest, and Annie Abbot and herself tying him firmly round the neck with a very woolly stocking. And there was Doctor Justin entering. Why! it was only five years ago, and yet how much younger he had looked then than he did nowadays. Different altogether, with more spring in him. Mrs. Brushett had never noticed any change in him until this minute. It disturbed her in a vague way. Then she saw him cross the room, briskly remove the stocking, and give them orders never to replace it. (How well she remembered that and how she, herself, had wound it comfortingly back again, once his steps had echoed down the stairs!) She had not felt guilty then, but now, oddly enough, she did. It made her stir a little uncomfortably as she thought of her friend, the Knight of Castile (a perfect gentleman if ever there was one) watching with her the deception that followed after. But lo! there before her very eyes, the impossible took place, and she saw herself persuading Mrs. Abbot of the uselessness of such a course—coaxing Edgar Alf into the belief that he was better without it—better with an open window than a shut one. Yes, and as day followed day upon the pageant of the screen, she saw herself, the fond, the weak, transformed into the strong, the wise. Was Edgar Alf in trouble over the matter of stolen milk bottles from the flat below, or door ringing in the streets nearby? Did she smother him with reproaches and kisses? No! there she was, firm and far seeing. Truly, Edgar Alf, the despot, had no chance against her on the screen. And now that there was less spoiling from her, curiously, there seemed to be less scolding from Annie Abbot. And how could he, their idol, catch cold as the years rolled by, when neither she nor Annie coddled him; how could he shirk his homework when she was there alert and eager to watch him do his nightly bit?

As in a dream Mrs. Brushett saw Edgar Alf grow from childhood into boyhood, from boyhood into young manhood— watched him struggling through the murk of London winters to night school, saw him gain a scholarship, and pass at last under the tall archway of the Technical College.

Then six months passed by on the screen. She and Annie were aging. Yes, aging obviously, but what did that matter when there was Edgar Alf, upright and pleasantly aggressive in his mechanic's overalls? There in that great domed place, the engineering yard, she saw him passing fearlessly among all the intricacies, all the dangers of wildly spinning wheels. She caught the gleam of steel, the twist of lathes, the drip of oil, all the orderly confusion of the bulky place. And lo! Edgar Alf moving among these sinister machines with an almost impudent indifference, his cap on the back of his head, a grease mark smearing his chin.

Then Edgar Alf messing about in the parlor at home with screws and bolts and a funny machine that leaked oil on to the carpet. And Mrs. Abbot following him closely up with newspapers and a stream of reproaches, and Edgar Alf with the passage of the days growing surly—nay, more than surly—rude. Mrs. Brushett held her breath. It pained her that the tall Knight should see him at this disadvantage.

"His father," she whispered in the confiding dark of the Grand Bohemian Cinema de Luxe, "his father coming out in him."

"Quite!" said the tall Knight, nodding. "Quite."

The screen flashed with drama as Edgar Alf was seen finally to fling the newspapers to the four corners of the room, and to spread himself, his screws, his bolts, his oil still more generously over the carpet and the table. Then behold! there was that screen heroine, Bella Brushett, tiptoeing to her bedroom, clearing away the chest of drawers, and moving the bed to the drafty end of the room—and lastly beckoning to Edgar Alf to enter into possession! This, again, she was pained to notice, he did less as a hero of films and more as a matter of course. One month passed, and lo! the bedroom of Mrs. Brushett was seen to become less and less a chamber of repose, and more and more a rather inconvenient-looking laboratory. When ten o'clock drew near, Mrs. Brushett watched herself make tentative suggestions that the hour for sleep had come, but the scowl of concentration on the brow of Edgar Alf seemed to contradict such whims on her part, and as the weeks passed by there she was slipping into Annie's bed.

"What does he think we are?" she watched Mrs. Abbot sardonically inquire. "The night shift or a blessed dancing club?" "Now, now," she saw herself comfortingly reply, "it's always something at that age—and you know it might so easily have bin drink or billiards, or something pricey like whippets."

And Part Two of the Life of Edgar Alf flickered across the screen in letters of light, and there he was at three of a winter's morning, waking them both out of their bed, a-kissing of them, and a-slapping of them on the back as if he were demented until Mrs. Annie Abbot, looking long and grim and rather like a bogey in a flannel nightgown, got up to sober him with a brew of strong black tea. And there he was a-swilling of it down, and a-jumping up and down his workroom a-gloating over all the mess he'd made and calling out enough to rouse the next door tenants. "I've a-done it! I've a-done it! And no one's ever done it quite the same before."

The next morning, a Thursday, instead of getting into his overalls at six o'clock, there he was at ten a-washing to his waist as if it was a Sunday, and a-dressing in his new plus fours.

"You'll be sacked, as sure as fate," Mrs. Abbot prophesied with melacholy distinctness.

"As sure as fate!" he answered roaring with laughter, "that I will! So pack up your troubles in your old kit bag, for we're leaving here a month today." And out he went—a-whistling down the Euston Road as if he owned the station. . . . In the darkness of the theatre Mrs. Brushett sighed indulgently. What a one he was! The next minute she started, for on the screen before her the words shone forth, "One Month Later," and there, sure enough, were she and Mrs. Abbot, in a tremendous flutter, packing up the family trunk—and what was more astounding, the climax you might say to a life spent in tubes and buses, there were they both driving from that well-known door in a brand-new orange taxi, with all the neighbors looking on. . . . Feverishly Mrs. Brushett clutched the tall Knight's elbow, as the taxi buzzed through north London towards the west for more than half an hour, and stopped at Ealing Common outside a little red brick house with four holly bushes in the garden and the name "Laburnam Lodge" painted distinctly on the fanlight of the door.

And there inside the taxi was Annie Abbot, the self-possessed and aggressive, clutching at her hand as timid as a child, and saying nervously again and yet again, "I only 'opes he came by it honest—for it don't seem natural, no it don't." And she herself exclaiming exultantly, "Well, now, if this ain't an Occasion!" for there was Edgar Alf, hands in pockets, legs astride, looking jauntily at ease within the open doorway, and shouting "Welcome Home!" Wreathed in smiles she watched herself follow Mrs. Abbot, who very genteely picked her way down the little pebbled path, a tiny flush upon her hard gray cheek.

Six blissful months passed on the screen before their eyes, in the little house at Ealing, with Edgar Alf working every day and nearly every night, and Mrs. Brushett and Mrs. Annie Abbot buying umbrellas and such like luxuries and having the first rest of their lives.

"It's almost too good to be true!" whispered Mrs. Brushett to the Knight of Castile.

"Wait and see," said he, and again the screen flashed, and there was Edgar Alf one evening grumbling that the house

was too small, his workroom too small, that his firm was too small, yes, and London too small. . . . Mrs. Brushett gasped as she watched him waving his arms and talking crossly of scope. If this wasn't a-tempting of Providence. Every minute she expected to see her beloved struck down, but he wasn't. He simply became more peevish, and built a garage in the garden. This done he bought a field that lay on their other side, and built there a large roomy workshop and spent another three months fitting it up with all the latest improvements. And when *that* was completed, and he admitted his satisfaction, he came down to breakfast next morning, and said he was off to America, as there, there was plenty of room.

The weeks that followed then upon the screen were painful to behold, but to the admiration of the onlookers in that darkened cinema below, that screen heroine, Bella Brushett, never faltered once. Tirelessly in private, she cautioned Edgar Alf, tirelessly in private, she sought to inspire the spirit of the pioneers in Mrs. Annie Abbot until at last she'd paved the way for him, and stood with her upon that long, sad platform at Waterloo to say goodby to Edgar Alf.

And there he was a-nodding gaily to them from the window, and looking as confident as a chauffeur and talking up to the last minute of all the scope there was abroad, and that new engine that in time he meant to build—an engine that would forge its way across both the treacherous sandy places of the desert, and the tangled growths of jungle.

"Well, Alf," said Mrs. Abbot briefly, "don't get ate up one day there when you're thinking about something else!" But her chin trembled as she spoke. Mrs. Brushett from the darkness of the cinema felt her heart contract. There she and Annie were, gray-haired, growing older, weaker daily, she and Annie who had done everything for him, and there he was, gay-like, going off as if America was Clapham Common. And never once it seemed to strike him that they might never see him again. There they both were, longing to tear him out of that railway carriage, to clasp him in their arms, to cry, "Never, never, Today is all we ever have." But they didn't, for it wouldn't have been the thing. Neither of them knew exactly what it was, the thing, nor that the dignity of both their weary lives was somehow built on what the thing had always cost them. They only knew they must stand there and do nothing, while there he stood, using up the few remaining minutes with talk of scope and engines. . . . In the darkness of the cinema, something fierce rose up in Mrs. Brushett for the first time in her life as she watched the screen, something as old as love, as strong as hate. Almost she felt she could strike that smile of Edgar Alf's. Didn't he know, couldn't he see, it was the last minute they'd ever have together. . . .

But there before her on the screen, facing the public, Mrs. Brushett smiled and nodded, standing rather close to Annie Abbot. The ticket collecter slammed the door finally. Her very heart seemed to close in on itself. Her knees were trembling oddly.

The guard blew his whistle shrilly. On the shrill blast of it she saw herself raise her head and look at Edgar Alf with the pain of a hundred memories imprisoned behind her washed-out eyes. "God," she began, "God bless . . ."

Edgar Alf stopped short as the train jerked back. His face paled suddenly as if in a flash the truth had dawned on him.

"Mother!" he cried, leaning out towards them both. "Mother . . . I . . ." but they never caught his message in the gathering speed of the train. Together they stood there stupidly, long after it had vanished into that tragic, magic space, thin air, whither so many of the proud beloveds of this sad earth go—two trembling old women, one with a nervous smile, and the other a stiff upper lip, until all the passers-by streamed past them, until the unheard signal box went klick-klack, and Mrs. Brushett turned her head, knowing now at last for her the two-thirty well away . . .

In the kindly darkness of the cinema she bowed her head upon a handkerchief. "I can't look any more," she whispered through her tears, "tell me what happened to him afterwards."

"He became a very famous man," said the Knight of Castile quietly, as he led her from the cinema. "Yes, a very famous man, at an astonishing early age. But he did not become a great man until quite late in life . . ." the Knight paused. "Latterly he had a good deal of pain and trouble through his son. He was very like himself you see."

In the daylight once more Mrs. Brushett blinked. The Knight put a steadying arm round her shoulders. "His was a life full of noble achievement," he said.

"Would have bin," said Mrs. Brushett sadly, "if I 'adn't bin that silly with him."

"Come, come," said the tall Knight cheerfully, "this is your great Day Off, so none of your melancholies now." And he waved his gauntlet glove towards a brand-new hansom that came spanking past.

"Well! if this ain't like old times," said Mrs. Brushett obediently gulping her tears, "seeing one of these back—all as cosy and compact as a h'arm chair locomoting. Where are we bound for now?

"Home!" said the Knight of Castile, leaping in after her in his distinguished way.

"Home!" said Mrs. Brushett wonderingly, as they bowled along a great avenue of chestnut trees, pitching their shadows like tents beneath them. "Home! where can that be now?"

"See," said the Knight beside her, "how the avenue gradually darkens. The sun has set, we have come to the last milestone. Behold!"

And leaning across the hansom door Mrs. Brushett beheld at last under steeply sloping tiles of the very finest quality, the dream house rich in innumerable latticed windows and countless cosy corners, set squarely in the ideal garden, its white enameled gate outstretched in welcome, and the whole little plot encircled by a ring of brightest gold.

"Every woman," said the Knight of Castile dreamily, "every woman sees her future home in her engagement ring."

Mrs. Brushett caught her breath. This was her very own. Even if he had not told her, she would have recognized it anywhere. The house she had always planned, the house she had always known was hers if only she could reach it. As she stared enraptured at it, the shadows deepened; little waves of scent from stock and mignonette drifted towards them, on the moist, warm air; sparrows rustled nervously for a moment in the leaves above them, then drowsed asleep again with a sleepy twitter of protest; then silence seemed to pour out of the vast silent places of the heavens on the Knight and Mrs. Brushett, like a cooling benediction, until somewhere in a woody place, very near the earth, an owl hooted distantly.

Suddenly, at that moment a lamp was lit within the dream house, and a shadow fell upon the blind. Mrs. Brushett sat very still, almost as still as death.

"Get down," said the Knight of Castile, "he is waiting."

"Terry," Mrs. Brushett breathed, "Terry."

"Naturally," said the Knight, "whom else did you expect?"

Tremblingly Mrs. Brushett rose to her feet. In the dim light, although he could not see, the Knight of Castile knew that her cheek was flushed, her vague eyes dewy bright, and that she was once more twenty-five.

Then as her feet touched the ground, she suddenly stopped. "What'll happen to Edgar Alf? Tell me that?" she besought him. "Couldn't I send Annie Abbot a message of warning?"

The tall Knight shook his head. "The lines of communication between the Earth World and the Country of Tomorrow are not yet established. Edgar Alf must take his chance."

"But he ain't never had it!" she cried. "Can't I go back for a bit to warn him?"

"You have not yet crossed the threshold," said the tall Knight, "and so I suppose you can. But it means you postpone your own happiness. I suppose you have thought of that?"

"No, I ain't," said Mrs. Brushett firmly, "I ain't, and I ain't going to. If I do, I know I shan't." And she turned back into the waiting hansom. "If this is real—it'll keep I expec'—but somehow I don't feel that Edgar Alf will."

"Think twice," counseled the Knight very gravely.

"I can't, and I won't!" she cried desperately, bursting into a terrible flood of tears, then, blindly raising the tiny trap door behind her, she called loudly and wildly, "Home!"

And now she seemed to sink back into darkness, a darkness that soothed to begin with and blotted out all her tears in exhaustion—until gradually as this lessened, it seemed to grow lighter and lighter, full of small fussy sounds that pulled and teased her attention in a dozen different directions.

"That's better!" she heard the tall Knight say, "a great deal better. Now open your eyes." And she was back in the cupboard room, high over the Euston Road, and Doctor Justin bending over her, a pucker between his two dark brows. Dazedly, yet clearly, she noted the wide-flung window behind him, and a damp splash of water trickling over the window sill, and an earthen jug empty of rose-colored lilies.

"Come, now! That's better," he repeated, no longer in

the brisk tones usual to him, but gently, as if he were welcoming her back from a long and tiring journey. "What do you mean by sealing yourself like this in an expensive atmosphere of orchids?" and he laid a long, sharp needle on a white cloth by her bed.

Helplessly she gazed up at him. Her wrist pained her for some reason, and she did not follow his words. Her mind was full of her past experience.

"Doctor!" she said, no longer in awe of him, strong in the candor of awakening consciousness. "Doctor," she said, "I've bin in the Valley of the Shadow all afternoon, I have."

"Well, well," and he patted the hand that did not hurt, the hand in which, tightly clenched, lay the heathenish amulet. "You're back at any rate. Perhaps now you'll realize you're not really a hothouse plant."

"Doctor," she said, staring at him with a new steadiness. "I were just in sight of heaven."

The Doctor started a little. Then, "What was it like?" he asked curiously, as friendly like as any Knight of Castile.

Mrs. Brushett's eyes misted over slightly with the effort to define it. "It's difficult to tie it down," she said hesitatingly, "but it wasn't a bit strange. That was the funny thing. It was somehow just like Greenwich Park on a fine Sunday morning years and years ago."

The doctor nodded thoughtfully, with that momentary compression of the lips so usual to him. "Quite," he said, slowly, "quite," and he stared hard into the faded bed quilt, and again Mrs. Brushett noticed how much older he seemed since that day he had so firmly unwound Edgar Alf from the warmth of the woolly black stocking.

She felt suddenly very sorry that this was so. She felt she must tell him this—and then just as suddenly she knew she could not. She lay back upon her pillows, smiling weakly in a silly way, and feeling strangely defeated. Then they heard Annie's step outside.

"And remember," he stood there by the door, tall, and alert and worn, smiling his charming, seldom smile. "You're not nearly ready for heaven yet. We're going to keep you for many a long year still."

"That's true!" Mrs. Brushett started forward, "that's true, doctor," she said very earnestly, "I could have stayed, but I didn't. It's difficult to boil it down to words, but I had to come back for Edgar Alf. I remembered him just at the very last minute. I only got back in time—by the skin of my teeth, you might say." . . .

Man of
the Moment

Man of the Moment

Scarlet tunics blazed from the London bandstand. Baskets of bright geraniums festively bobbed in the first zephyr of the heat-wave summer evening. The cloudless sky was dusky gold above the idle grass—already the enclosure was packed. All park seats within hearing were tightly wedged with warm bodies in reluctant proximity. In the sixpenny chairs, cigarettes were feverishly smoked by a post-war people defenseless against the vast interrogation of an empty moment. An overflow from the back seats stood in a dense crowd awaiting the conductor's first appearance.

An impressive figure in a dark double-breasted tunic, gold shoulder knot, peaked cap, white gloves strode down the center aisle, and mounted the rostrum. Very much the man of the moment.

"It's a different one tonight!"

"Fine figger of a man."

"But older than you'd expect?"

"Stylish all the same."

Ineffably elegant, authority itself, the conductor tapped his baton, and a march *Trombones to the Fore* smote the summer night. They were off! Beneath his delicate yet inflexible hand, excitement was conjured and discharged pell-mell. During *The Gondoliers,* apathy fell away. The front chairs quickened. Satisfaction overtook the critical back seats. He was the genuine article. This was something like the thing! Not too many movements either! You could read him like an open book. Plenty of flow. Subduing the brass, coaxing the clarinets, beckoning the oboe, cajoling the flute, summoning the horns! Everybody's time was coming. Meantime the music made itself plain.

Gazing into the empty apricot sky, expansiveness became the order of the departing day. There was a bland benevolence abroad. Difficulties eased off, or were heroically met in *Pomp and Circumstance.* Life wasn't so bad after all. Unless we went to war again—*Tannhäuser* came later in the pink penny program. Oh, well, it might rain tomorrow! Better make the most of this.

A lady and a gentleman had walked right up to the front row of the sixpennies—what a hope! But the attendant had snapped open two green seats. That was money for you! A big burly gent in an export suiting, starched collar and cuffs—with a slim dark piece in tow . . . no jewelery but looked a million. Black outfit too smart for mourning. Must be a foreigner, although *he* was British right enough.

Relentlessly the sixpennies studied her during the band's next breather. Older than you'd think at first. Thirty at least. Actress, dancer, singer? They were at a loss. They could not place her. An elderly man who had once seen service at home and abroad with that lost legion, the Upper Ten, came nearest to it. But what was she doing with that industrialist? The usual thing, he supposed.

The conductor raised his immaculately gloved hand. He tapped his baton imperatively, and his twenty-four scarlet bandsmen surged into Strauss's waltz as one man. The faces on each side of the latecomers, inimical earlier from uncertainty, relaxed again. That romantic tunic, ordaining, directing, decreeing! The crowd grew nostalgic, indulgent. He was their idea of an Imperial hussar—

But he was not the Austrian lady's! Negligently she dismissed him and his music—if only they knew how yellow the beautiful Blue Danube was! Feverishly she was thinking of the man at her side: *"If he doesn't propose tonight he never will!"* He would just be one more of those big bluff men who were all over the place, but never on the spot—men of the moment only. A week ago she could have sworn that he was serious when he took her to see over that empty house beyond Hampstead. "How would this place strike a woman?" It had struck her dumb. Vivid lawns, glossy shrubs, velvet roses—a garden like a freshly embroidered sampler. Leafy rooms that faced due south; a small bright kitchen; a large refrigerator in a tall, tiled scullery. Below the slates in her own hot bed-sitting room, off Baker Street, milk soured overnight as a matter of course and town lettuces, nursed in a bowl of tepid water, wilted in an hour. The only thing that stood up to that inferno of a room was these orchids he'd sent yesterday. And orchids were an extravagance from a Midlands man that did not augur permanence.

Politely she continued to stare into space. How did this place strike a woman? As hollow as an echo. A bandstand evoking endless others. Fashionable spas abroad where she and her aunt had clung tooth and nail to their own set—up to the eleventh hour. Back bedrooms in better-class hotels, then front rooms in second-rate ones—thereafter the descent had been rapid until her aunt's death. *How would this house strike a woman?* Not a word had been said since! Probably he meant to install a housekeeper.

Then why was he still hanging around? Was he finding it difficult to put a less flattering offer before her? Well, there he'd drawn a blank, did he but know. Max had proved the only awakening she'd ever require there! No monkey-tricks—her grandmother's deadly phrase had cut at the roots of promiscuity long ago. A terrifying old lady to have sole charge of a child, but with a wry gratitude she often now remembered her words. This post at the modiste's wouldn't last forever, but she still had three languages. She could always get a job. Soon he would disappear. A pity she always got fond of anyone if she saw them regularly. Affectionate rather than passionate she supposed. Or was she simply tired? As long as she kept her health she would keep on working. Her health . . . she must just hope for the best. No, hope was dead about everything. Faith only was left—if faith was this pale wraith, this acid specter of determination that now stood for her self.

Icily she smiled as the band breezed buoyantly through a naval medley.

The burly man beside her frowned. Shouldn't have brought her here. Not smart enough. Give her a wrong impression. As a rule he found her silence pleasing. For all her poise she was a quiet lass. But tonight he was uneasy. Was she bored with him after all? The dark hair snooding her pale brow, her eloquent eyes, her slender hands were the expression of a fastidious something that fascinated, and yet intimidated him. Her distinction drew him yet defied him until now Midlands pride turned traitor in diffidence. Money talked he knew, but for the first time in his experience, his left him silent. Yet if he didn't look alive someone else would snap her up. But if she refused him? Safest to play for time. A fellow had to be certain he was on the right tack before he committed himself—otherwise he looked a fool.

Restlessly he moved on his inadequate chair, and was again snared by her small pale ear—intricate, ageless as a shell. So silent, yet so alive for him—this smooth little statue of a creature! The one woman—world without end.

The naval medley rollicked to its close. The conductor turned to acknowledge the applause. Saluting smartly, his was no longer the austerity of a military hero. He was smiling with a touch of that daredevil gallantry popularly associated with the Senior Service.

"Gets every ounce out of his men," observed the Midlands man. "Bright and breezy, devil-may-care—that's how the ladies like them, isn't it?"

"That man?" despairingly she stared at the conductor for the first time. "How can you say such a thing? That man is tragic. Look at the grooves from his nose to his mouth. He's got a duodenal ulcer—but its only part of the misery. He's really a first-class musician. Can't you see he's come down in the world—that its dreadful he should be dressed up like that."

"By jove, you're right," the Midlands man took another look at the conductor's scholarly profile. "Yes, poor devil, he's been through quite a bit. But how did you know?" Almost accusingly he turned upon her.

A trifle wildly she exclaimed: "I can read the lines in his face—something in his air. I've been hungry too."

His face crimsoned. "Hungry—*you?*"

She gave a scornful little laugh. Truth was risky but she was past caring. "Oh, I've never starved. But I've often been hungry. The best meals I've had for years have been those you've given me these five weeks." Listlessly she glanced from the dusty, beaten ground at her feet to the fading sky, now milky as a dying opal.

The man beside her sat speechless. In a split second the visible universe had recast itself. He and she were safely marooned with this stark fact that was salvation. Benevolence, long repressed, but sanctioned at last, intoxicated him. Yet his hand trembled on the program—exquisite as a butterfly she might even now take wings.

His frantic attention focused on the pink sheet. Seven had always been his lucky number: *Perchance to Dream.* Swiftly he drew out his fountain pen, and effaced one word. Dumbfounded by the originality of his idea he inserted instead, at white heat, another in block letters, buttressed by a towering question mark. Compassion had routed self-consciousness. *Perchance to Wed?* Urgently he thrust this before her.

Astounded she gazed from the program to his face, which had now paled surprisingly. Beneath the forcible intent of his desperation her own gaze dropped.

"Thank you," she breathed, "I shall be very glad. . . ." And in his blind relief the unsuitability of this humble reply completely escaped him. They were both saved. Everything was all right now. A-1 at Lloyds!

Lights sprang on. The pavilion shone whitely, but fairy lamps like large commercial glowworms richly festooned the shrubs. The pale sky now flowed clear and swift as water, shadows below clean-cut as the ace of spades.

One of the back seats gave a sudden curse. "Will you look at that!"

"Look at what?"

"At the conductor, you ijut! If it isn't his holy high and mightiness Handy Andy!"

"*What?* Never!"

"As sure as death—saw 'im the minute the light snapped on. Quick—he's turning now!"

"Gawd, Bill, you're right! Well, who'd have thought it!" Her spleen was caressing in its reminiscence. Calculation stalked at ease. "My, what a facer for 'im, if *she'd* come after all tonight. Him in his white gloves—stuck up there, like a blasted gentleman. S'pose it ud be too late to nip over for her now?"

"And lose our seats—just to find her sozzled!"

"Didn't want to lose *him*—that's all."

"What's your hurry? There's always tomorrow isn't there?"

"You bet your life there is! He's in the bag—"

The conductor tapped his baton. The summer zephyr had become a fitful shiver from the southwest. For a moment he felt upon his triumph a chill breath, a graying of the heart. Then the music reclaimed, restored him. He and the boys were spanking into Sousa. Sammy (drums and cymbals) had warned him that they were a sticky lot. But at both rehearsals they'd answered like a bell. From the word go—all well disposed to him, ready to do their best! When he thought of some of the toughs he'd licked into shape . . . but these fellows were fully trained. This was *Excelsior!* Under the baton he knew the boys as they knew their instruments. Sammy was easing up—Sammy his blooming mascot, for ever putting this or that in his way. But never before had anything like tonight been possible. All his life had been an ascent to this moment. He was past the age for miracles which made it more remarkable. "Blaze away!" Sammy had said.

Blaze away, Handy Andy, the son of Ash-bin Andy, the local garbage man! Council cleaners they were called today but he'd bet that a pig pail still smelled the same! Yet even in that refuse heap music had been waiting for him—in the first mouth

(209

organ his father had salvaged for him. Then choir practice, Boys'
Brigade, cinema orchestra—Works' band. . . .

The Works' band in Birmingham, under his first baton,
had been his only success. Big money. It had bought Milly and
sold him! *Stars and Stripes*—to this very refrain she and her
bachelor Billiards King had later hopped it. Though it meant
losing the band, he had beat it too—thankful to cut his losses in
this escape from her. To get out when the going was good! Sus-
picious, it struck him that they'd never asked for divorce. Welsh
Miners Unemployment Band . . . Street Band . . . Second
World War . . . Factory Band—the climb to the heights had
begun again. Through thick and thin, every type of employment
he'd hung on to any kind of band. He'd never lost sight of his
instruments. Agents in Earl's Court and Shepherd's Bush knew
him to be punctual as the other fellow's pint—but stone sober
himself . . . his ulcer saw to that. And as often as not something
turned up. But never before a chance like this. This was it, and
no mistake!

Sousa subsided in *Reverie.* The microphone was his terror.
His accent always gave him away. But here there was no need
to announce the items. That number board saved his face. His
luck was in at last. He was to finish the week too, and it might
lead to something else. Next year was Coronation year. Good
things were on their way. After *Tannhäuser* now, he would turn
and conduct his first London audience in "God Save the Queen."

Superbly he waited while the score was changed for him.

Watching the piccolo's nimble fingers in this service,
compassion surprised him. These twenty-four good men and true
were but himself at different stages. The tap of his baton for the
last item was an invocation to a gathered experience. This was
Tannhäuser's triumph—the dried stick flowering.

His white gloves flashed, his gold braid shone. The gray

blight lifted in the first clash of the cymbals. With arms incisive and hips gaunt beneath his tunic—disciplined elegance itself, he launched himself upon his moment. To his amazement he found it expanding . . . with a generosity that was gratitude, or a gratitude that was generosity. He didn't have to make the most of it any more. It had made the most of him.

In sonorous safety the cymbals clashed again, releasing Wagner. Music was the complete get-away, because everything was marshaled in it—nothing was scamped.

Yes, tonight beneath his baton revelation was on the march!

Master Craftsman

Master Craftsman

He was a small, alert man of ninety when first I met him in 1948, blessed with the full use of all his faculties, and had ridden a bicycle daily until he was eighty. He confessed that he had now taken to spectacles for reading, and that he didn't read as much as once he had—it took him all his time to get through the newspapers, but he still enjoyed Mr. Priestley. I discovered that his voluntary work during the last war had been the extinction of "local incendiaries."

Queen Victoria had been a vigorous matron of thirty-nine when he was born. Mr. John Henry (to give him two of his three names) made his appearance in the wake of the Crimean War, when England had found herself allied with France for the first time in two centuries. Disraeli, Gladstone, Nightingale were the household names in those days: gin and beer palaces, and Moody and Sankey meetings the street sensations. He was twenty-six when Kartoum fell.

Like his father before him, he was a worker in leather— "not the finicking things, but the big stuff." Military portmanteaux that would hold a sword. One speciality was traveling cases for the Indian princes—leather so richly studded with precious stones that it had to be kept in a bank while it was being worked. Reluctantly he would admit that things had not been easy in his youth. His father, although a good worker, had not had his advantages, but had been determined that his son should be a master craftsman. There had been sacrifices. In short, to enumerate the changes that the trade had seen in Mr. John Henry's lifetime would be to write the history of his century.

In his day the craftsman made his own thread, and thereby hung romance! Bundles of hemp reached the workers from a firm in Scotland. The lassies there would slip in messages to the lads receiving them. Letters were often exchanged. Mr. John Henry sent informative pictures of the Tower Bridge and other sites of civic importance. One maiden went the length of asking for his photograph instead. Mildly he shook his head in answer to my question: "That would have been carrying a joke too far—I didn't write again."

His memory was phenomenal—to him the Boer War was as yesterday. He gave his views on any subject with the reticence of a vast experience, but his statements had the precision of authority. His brow was domed, the eyes direct in gaze, the transparent lids shadowed, their melancholy belied by a sagacious nose and a humorous mouth. His hands were the most remarkable I have ever seen. In youth these must have been singularly beautiful, but now the fingers, still incredibly agile, were so strenuously knotted at the joints that the hands could not fold. Their vitality was such that when motionless they gave the impression that they were resting Mr. John Henry. When they lay upon his knee or the table they resembled musical instruments of some strange sort, or twin skulls that spoke a language of their own. Two fingers of his right hand had been "hobbled" early in his career, and never again straightened. A mate's knife had slipped. He agreed that this had hampered him at first, but assured me that later he had never noticed hindrance.

Our first meeting was unusual. On a November Sunday I saw him, a small, frail figure in cap and muffler waiting on a seat in Finchley Road, staring into space. Despite my hurry, I was impelled to turn back, and sit down beside him. He had taken the wrong bus, and was just having a breather before he climbed over the hill to the Marie Curie Hospital. His wife was there. . . . The impression Mr. John Henry made on me was such that I found it hard to leave him. We exchanged addresses. That was the start of our friendship.

At Christmas time I received a greeting card of a candle twinkling amid stars, with a message that he had some news for me which he would give me later. At the close of the festive season, and not till then, he sent the news: his wife had died.

When Mr. John Henry came to call he did not wear his cap and muffler. He wore a bowler hat and a black silk scarf, and he carried a walking stick in his ungloved hand. In my room that first day the *Times* lay at his elbow, with some other newspapers. "As a union man—" he said, and indulgently shook his head. On my return, bearing our tea, I found him politely toying with the Thunderer.

Shortly before his death in his ninety-first year, he found to his surprise that he could not rise. His relations called a doctor, for Dad's independence was such that weakness would destroy him. Something had to be done at once.

The doctor drew aside his son and intimated that his father was now dying of old age.

"But age had nothing to do with Dad," his son insisted, exasperation in his voice, and on second thought I too could but agree. Mr. John Henry's circle was, in fact, dumbfounded by his death, for when integrity prevails, it prevails to some purpose.

Returning later from the funeral service that sunny Saturday afternoon (Mr. John Henry still moving abreast of the century had elected to be cremated), Waterloo Road had one of those bright, mute moments that occur when the workers have gone home at mid-day, and I reflected that, true to tradition, he had not only finished his work, he had finished the week, and again knocked-off at the appointed hour.

Crossing Waterloo Bridge, the river sparkling, I paused.

The sky was cloudless. King's Reach had never seemed so regal.

All that was mortal of Mr. John Henry was now a pinch of dust, but there rose his London: Westminster at that hour veiled in its own shadow; to the right the City, a-dazzle; St. Paul's, a dome of light, and all standing proudly—as well they might.

March Cost

March Cost's work was best described by Stewart Hunter, the Scottish critic, when he wrote: "March Cost's work suggests the tranquility and depths of a loch, in which strange and lonely skies lie mirrored. To savor this quality of mystery, of atmosphere, of an external world constantly penetrated by rumors of another, I would especially recommend *The Bespoken Mile*."

Critics have been looking for superlatives to describe Miss Cost's work since her first novel, *A Man Named Luke,* was published in 1932. This book caused one New York newspaper to run the headline: "Mrs. Roosevelt Flies With A Man Named Luke."

Her second novel, *The Dark Glass,* moved Professor Loiseau, of the University of Bordeaux, in a monograph on her work, to write: "Her landscapes are those of a poet and her prose has rightly been praised as a model of harmony . . . in the mysterious zone on the borders of life and the beyond, her originality finds its full confirmation."

Miss Cost, who was born Margaret Mackie Morrison in Glasgow, Scotland, is the eldest member of a family of writers. From an early age she evidenced a keen interest in the arts. Between the ages of nine and seventeen she studied drawing, painting, and sculpture at the Glasgow School of Art. Later she studied dramatic art and toured with Sir Frank and Lady Benson's company. After she left the theater, Miss Cost traveled widely. Her journeys have taken her throughout Europe and across the United States. Her sister, N. Brysson Morrison, is known to American audiences as the biographer of Mary Stuart and Henry VIII; her

(219

brother, T. J. Morrison, is a novelist and film writer; another brother, John Morrison, is a poet and novelist; and her sister, Mary Morrison, is known for her short stories.

In her study near the charming spa, Tunbridge Wells, March Cost has produced a dazzling succession of novels. These include *The Dark Star; The Hour Awaits,* which was a Book-of-the-Month Club selection; *I, Rachel,* her moving re-creation of the great nineteenth century French actress, Rachel, and her world; and *The Countess,* which was her first venture into American history. This latter novel tells the story of Sir Benjamin Thompson, the noted eighteenth century American-born scientist, who was created Count Rumford, and of his daughter, Sarah, Countess Rumford. Her most recent success is the delightful comedy of manners, *The Year of the Yield.*

Cost
Period pieces